Man Enough

ShivamVerma

Rajmangal Prakashan

An Imprint of **Rajmangal Publishers**

ISBN : 978-9390894857

Published by :

Rajmangal Publishers

Rajmangal Prakashan Building,
1st Street, Sangwan, Quarsi, Ramghat Road
Aligarh-202001, (UP) INDIA
Cont. No. +91- 7017993445

www.rajmangalpublishers.com

rajmangalpublishers@gmail.com

sampadak@rajmangalpublishers.in

प्रथम संस्करण : अप्रैल 2021

प्रकाशक : राजमंगल प्रकाशन

राजमंगल प्रकाशन बिल्डिंग, 1st स्ट्रीट,

सांगवान, क्वार्सी, रामघाट रोड,

अलीगढ़, उप्र. – 202001, भारत

फ़ोन : +91 - 7017993445

First Published : April 2021

eBook by : Rajmangal ePublishers (Digital Publishing Division)

Dedication

To friends and family that give meaning to my life.

To my amazing publisher, who never gives me a dull moment.

Lastly, to all the joy that i have been able to bring to my readers.

Table of Contents

Chapter 1

It was weekend, the time everybody waited for entire week to come, and wish to stay forever. City of Nightindale was usually calm on weekends. The men of the city were split into three when it came to weekends. One would still be sleeping over half of the day. Two would dedicate themselves to catch up with entire week's pending checklist. Three would greet the day with possibilities. This was the story of men in this city, or rather of every man in world. For Max, weekend was same as for all of these types. He would wake up late, and still call it a morning. He would tune to city's trendiest podcast while driving to mark off the checklist. And lastly the rest of weekend he would leave it for possibilities, for something unseen or unplanned.

It was noon and Max was rushing in. He had a very bloody important thing to do, for his fiancé. After all it was about her life. Stella wanted it badly, and Max was his man to do it. But Max was little scared, he was little obnoxious, he was not getting the right feeling to do this. But he had to. He was her man, and doing something for fiancé was still considered manly, though listening to her wasn't. But some men would disagree, as listening and doing went hand in hand.

He had to reach Châteaux à l'ombre, yeah that was little French, but it was what her wife wanted. For past 25 minutes, Max had been circling around the same spot. It was damn confusing. He didn't wanted to step out, reach out another man and ask for direction. He had trust on his abilities, and didn't give up looking. The Google map had no directions to this place, neither did other maps had. It has to be this way, as such places were always off the grid. Stella's call came in and he stopped.

Stella said, "It hardly takes 30 minutes, and you have been out for last 1 hour. Where are you? I cannot go there by myself, you know that. Couldn't you find that place?".

Max exhaled, "Just there. Okay, I see a familiar face, let me ask him where is this place.".

Max stepped out of car and said, “Hey could you give me directions to Chateaux à l'ombre. By the way, I have seen you somewhere.”.

The stranger smiled, “Not somewhere, but exactly at that bus stop, while you drove through this street three times. By the way, Chateaux à l'ombre is right there in the fifth red color building.”.

There it was, without any address sign, shaded by trees, a huge black door. Max stepped inside, and there was nobody but huge boxes packed up lying in all corners of the room. The light was dim, and Max knew that this was the place where his fiancé wanted him to be. But seriously, they weren’t even married, and Max had to do such things, such despicable things. What would happen when they would get married, maybe some more rush, maybe some more secrets, maybe some more possibilities. But hell yes, Max would do it, for the woman he loved.

A lady called him from behind, “Hey, what is it you are looking for.”.

Max said, “Oh, I am looking for a fiancé. Oh, no, no, no. I am not looking for a fiancé, as I have one, and you too mam are so good to be my fiancé, I mean somebody’s fiancé. But I am here to save my wife from deadly diseases. Ah, you know, those savers of the day.”.

Lady sighed, “You mean tampons. It has to be, because this is what we sell.”.

Max smiled, “Of course, you won’t sell yourself just because you are in the store. I mean yeah, Tampons. Those small thingy things.”.

Lady whiffed and handed him a packed bundle, “Handle with care, they are radioactive too.”.

This was what a man had to do maintain the status quo with their opposites. Seriously, can’t Stella had walked the next door chemist to buy some of these radioactive things, but no she had to have the French handmade Tampons, and Chateaux à l'ombre in English meant Castle in the shade. Seriously the name was so apt, that it would hide all blood stains, and unhygienic serums in it. This was also a punishment in disguise of about to marry a woman who thinks she is a lady. Well but Stella couldn't know this, not that she is lady, but that Max doesn't thinks so. But seriously being a man wasn't easy, especially if you are out to buy tampons, because by doing so, you put entire reputation of all the men on stake. Buying Tampons was a taboo for men, it was like crime as heinous as crying during sex, and Stella made him do it. But wait, where Tampons really radioactive, if that so, Max's life had too got in danger. But it couldn't be, as clearly the woman on counter wanted to roast Max for not having checked her out. But why should he, when God had home delivered Victoria's secrets to his home. Well it wasn't god, but that young lad, who was more impressed with Stella than his brand's ambassadors. Max stepped out, and wait, was this man too from the bus stop. Yeah there was another familiar face right in front.

The other man said, "Whoa, is this place yours. I mean this Tampon factory. Max its me, Jordan.".

It did rang a bell and Max patted his back, "Of course I remember you missing your periods. Ah the college periods of course. and slowly Jordan, this isn't lottery ticket, its tampons, and men can't keep yelling Tampon, Tampon. And I don't own this place. In fact, if I'd be girl, id still not be making tampons, because I would be embarrassed on the fact what if I were a boy. I am a boy, I mean a man. But this is so not my place.".

Jordan trying to catch up with him said, "Yeah I understand, a man with a tampon is like a woman with a banana, because you don't know what to do with it. I am with you on it."

Max hugged him and then couldn't believe his eyes, "Fuck No, you own a Aston Martin DB9.".

Jordan turned back and smiles, "Oh yes, sometimes my wife gives the same expression. Is this yours?".

Max laughed and opened the door to see the interiors, "6000 cc, 6000 rpm power, 12 cylinder engine, this is a beast Jordan. Take it from me, don't leave you wife with it, or you will the get the expression, this has to be yours.".

Jordan said, "Yeah last thing I will do is leaving this beast with my wife, as its already endangered.".

Max chuckled, “Hey listen, why don’t you join us at our home. My fiancé, Stella would love to meet you. Not that she likes man company, but seeing a man like you is a rare feat. By the way, do you still wear undies straight for weeks, or they get to breath in our liberating city.”.

Jordan whiffed, “Not funny. By the way here is my card. Call me. But now I need to rush, or my wife will choke me with these tampons.”.

Everybody thinks that people change, but do they really. Max thought, not so. If one would stay with same people all their lives, Max would bet that they would see no change in them. But only if you met a person after a gap of year, or couple of years, you would be like, hey look at your beard, its longer than I last saw you. Of course it was longer, because in recent past that man didn’t have a shave and it had nothing to do with change. It hasn’t even been a year since Max had completed college, and he was here in the blooming city of Nightindale hustling day in day out. Bumping into old friends was one perk of living in large cities. Max belief in god became firmer, not because he just bumped into a close pal, but because he bumped into him with tampons, while Jordan too was there to buy tampons.

Doing something feminine is so death of manhood, but if you do it in a group, it dies within the circle. I mean Jordan wouldn’t tell anyone that while he was on to buy tampons he found Max with whole bunch of tampons. This was man logic. Max’s secret was safe. But seriously life was good for Max, what if he was driving an outdated sedan, it still had a very good conditioning that often froze his balls. It had a very good cushioning that Stella had appreciated quite many times while they got cozy. Though Max didn’t liked the timing of it, as he believed that Stella should show appreciation for other things of Max, and more to it Stella even did, she even showed appreciation for suspensions of the car. Anyways, Max loved every bit of his life. Wait, that poster can’t be true. ‘Men are Back’ starring Brooce Wills, whoa that badass baldy was back with a bang. This looked must watch, wait that must have to be a sign. He picked up his phone and called Stella.

Max said, “Hey honey, remember last night you said, it’s been ages we haven’t watched a movie.”

Stella said, “Yes, I did. And to that you said that world has stopped making great movies.”.

Max said, “You know what, God is always listening. Yes he did listen to us, and guess what I just saw a movie poster of Men are Back, starring Brooce Willis. I think we should hit the theaters. It will be lot of fun, and of course we wont be breaking the tradition of watching movies before marriage, like lovers do.”.

Stella snapped back, “But do you know what. I will prefer another set of ages of not having watched a movie. Men are back, seriously. You are the only man I want in my life. And do you think before marriage you should be showing me, knuckle chesters instead of rings, punches instead of kisses, whores instead of bridesmaid, and what not.”.

Max slowly said, “I think you are right. I hope god has listened to this one, so I will keep a watch.”.

Seriously giving her any ideas, was killing your own creativity. But then Men are back would also not suit much to a woman, so Max thought, if we were to wait for another age, why not hit men are back with some friends, well that too was a killer idea. What could be better than few beers down the throat and hitting the theatre. For now Max pulled in the alley of his house to deliver the life savers. The nightmare of delivering the tampons was done.

But wait, there was something more important to be done. Ah, what was most important in Max’s life was his family. I mean seriously what man would leave a girl half naked in bed, just to drive another 8 hours to reach home to see her sister’s just born daughter. Many would do, but most of them will spend another 1 hour with that half naked girl in bed, and take 9 hours before they saw their niece. But every second of Max was credited to his family. This Saturday too there was some family crisis, not that they were in danger, but sister had some business guest coming of Max’s brother in law, so someone had to pick the niece who had grown up to trouble her entire school. Yeah, like always she was a girl, she was attention hungry, and she also was a troublemaker. Today Uncle Max had to pick her from school. Max parked his car and went inside the classroom. It was not first time, so Max had expected the same too quirky too sexy to be a teacher in the room, who again smiled at Max. Seriously, why does all the good things happened when you are about to get married.

Max called, “Esther my girl, there she is. Wait, is she really riding on a boy. Hey Esther.”.

Esther turned back and said, “Uncle Max, will you become my donkey. I am not much heavy to be carried.”.

Max exhaled and looked back at the teacher, who was still smiling, Wait was she still smiling, or did she took a break while Max had eyes on Esther. God whatever, but some good chick was giving some damn good signals, that was for sure. Max kneeled down while children of the class started laughing.

Esther rode him and said, “Stop it guys, it is this donkey who will do the Hee Haw, Hee Haw.”.

Teacher interrupted, “Behave Esther. He is too good to do Hee Haw, I mean he is your uncle.”.

Max interrupted, “Ah, I got this. Esther, how do you talk to a donkey, tell everybody.”.

Esther started doing the Hee Haw, till Max took her on his shoulders to the car. Seriously, being a man, saving your reputation, and being with a kid was some of the nastiest things to do in this world. But deep in her heart, Esther loved Max way too much, to an extent, that It was only Max who became her donkey but not her father. And girls always loved the heavy lifting guys, and Esther was no exception. So these were the perks of this Saturday in Max’s life. Going to market, to pick the tampons, bumping into an old friend, then becoming a donkey for your niece.

Life was good, Max had everything he had ever wanted. Beautiful fiancé, two lovely sisters, a pretty niece, a fountain head brother, a father who always watched his back, and whole lot of family that got together every time anything good or bad happened in Max’s life. Max rode the car, while stopping three times to get Esther candies, ice cream, and more candies. This was what uncles were for, spoiling nieces. Back in home Daisy, Max's sister was busy serving brunch to Fred's, Max's brother in law, business partners. Seriously the glory of Saturday couldn't have been better with one of your family members kissing success. Max entered the house, while Esther rushed into Daisy's arms.

Daisy whispered, "I didn't knew that eating was also a serious business. Just look at them.".

Max smiled hugely in front of Fred and his business partner and said, "Oh, there is always more in life.".

Daisy nudged him and said, "He is my brother Max, soon to get married. Well, why didn't it occurred to me first. Maybe we should call you all to the marriage. You will have fun, and buns. Hey Esther, leave that bun.".

Max couldn't stop his laugh and went inside. Daisy followed and said, "Trust me Max, I will poison your kids, when you will have them. Oh, so that you don't have them.".

Max said, "Come on, It is just Ice cream. Even you used to feed me when I was kid. And its love.".

Esther interrupted, "Momma. Ice cream and lots of candies.". She smiled tearing her cheeks apart.

Daisy said, "God knows what will happen of this girl.".

Max held her hands while Daisy was caressing the washed clothes. "Look at us sis, aren't we doing fine, isn't life good, isn't there turkey in oven every thanksgiving, or do I look retarded with a captain cook eye, or I fumble every time I speak end up saying Hee haw, Hee haw.". He said that turning to Esther.

Fred entered with a knock for formality, "Max she is right. Girls of her age are learning symphony, not hee haw.".

Max snapped back, "Yeah, I don't wonder if you will build her an opera.".

Fred irritatingly said, "Least I am trying to build a better future for our family, and I haven't just sold myself to a corporate honcho. You know Daisy, who these people are, over their names. One is electoral candidate for our neighborhood council, the other is an Asian investor who is keen on investing in a housing scheme, the fat one is the biggest banker around, who really lends money to people like us, and not a venture capitalist with a poker face.".

Max said, "I think you should rephrase it, you are trying to build better homes for families like ours."

Max continued, "And that guy is not Asian. He is Chinese, and guess what your housing prices just went down.".

Daisy interrupted, "Hey, guys. I think someone should stop that fat banker from eating all cookies, seriously. And this is so about our girl Esther, it's her favorite ones.".

Max and Fred never got well together. The first reason was that how a job doing man and a business owner could probably adjust with each other. For Fred life was all about making new contacts, kissing on beautiful ladies cheeks, also complaining about the fact that his life was no more fun, then again making new contacts, finding new business opportunities.

On the other hand Max had always just wanted to live the life as it goes, and by the way, his life was all about his family and friends. The second reason was the same woman between them Daisy, to whom both pretended to love more than one another. But seriously, something was so wrong with Fred, I mean at an age when Esther was supposed to play in garden and parks, she was being taught on how to speak French. You know why, not because French was very popular as a language, but because anything taught at this tender age would go a long way. Seriously at this age and at this understanding, Esther would end up saying Merci every time a nice looking boy would try taking out her on a date. I mean Merci is good, but not in a very English way, I mean boy would be like, Excuse me.

He hated every time someone would treat Esther with candies, seriously what else a girl at her age is supposed to have, maybe a shot of vodka over a sophisticated book. Fred was so obsessed about his daughter, and her future, that he had even thought of sending her to one of the best boarding schools in the county. Well as an uncle, Max truly appreciated this move, but not the sentiments behind it. Fred wanted Esther to be in boarding school so she could make good contacts, and friends from high places, seriously, all this separation from family, so she could be a sidekick to someone else's family. These were the reasons that Max and Fred never got well together. Max was headed back home, and all he could think was his marriage. Seriously, what an emotion it was. Like a complete ban on seeing new girls, while you spend the rest of life with same woman. No more burgers, but only home made salad, because hunting days are gone man. But then Stella was something that Max always wanted.

Stella said, "Always on time you are. Its 8, I think I should undress.".

Max said, "Quicker the better, but that is only for undressing. One way, your way.".

Chapter 2

Seriously dining for men was simple, all you needed was a couple of beers and burgers or chicken wings or maybe a BBQ. But when it came to women, the dinner with your man has to be sophisticated. First there can't be beers, but only wine. Second there can't be anything native, so you will have to order something foreign something exotic, maybe Sushi, or maybe Thai soup. For Max, perks of getting engaged were not just confined to share bed with your opposite, but also sharing the bed sheet, sharing the pain it takes for cleaning that bed sheet. Yes Stella had already moved in, and as they wanted to spend this time together, make it special, and memorable forever.

Technically all Max was remembering for now was washing dishes together, ordering lingerie together which were meant to be worn after marriage, and like earlier this day buying tampons too. But then a man's life can never be bad, if you were to ask any one of them, so was with our Max. He would eat in the same plate as Stella did, and pretend there were no more extra dishes to wash. He would also add some spy flicks DVD's in the same cart as of Lingerie pretending that would be insightful to new exotic places, intentionally knowing how much Stella hated spy movies. And the tampons would save him from the country music that Stella played every night. This was life as fun for Max. To add some spice Stella had long planned this dinner date. If it weren't Stella, Max would tonight be going out with his friends and be served by waitresses with big booties. Obviously so Stella wanted the weekend to be Minimalist.

Max said, "Ah, I love this song. It reminds me of one of my friend, back in college.".

Stella frowned, "Oh Really, did she looked like Aria the singer who only wears two pieces regardless she is on a beach, or she is in a birthday party. By the way, recently her exotic photo shoot got featured in Men's Magazine that you often pick up with the groceries, the grosseries.".

Max said, "No, you get it all wrong. I pick that magazine for Carmen. Carmen the playmate.".

Stella took the menu and hit him, "So probably you should marry her and not me.".

Max said, "Remember when you were curious on our engagement day while I was busy on cell phone. Ah, I was sending a DM on twitter to Carmen. But it didn't work out."

Stella exhaled and unbelievably took out her cell phone to check her messages. Wait, she didn't had any other boyfriend or man other than Max, but clearly she was craving for more attention, while Max placed the order and was sipping wine while admiring the beauty of her fiancé. No he didn't said a word to her. It was the first rule of manhood, never praise a woman of her beauty until its required. At this time Max was no way going to get laid in this cozy restaurant, so he saved the likeliness of her hair streak colors to himself. Amidst the dim light of this restaurant there were many shining faces that Max could see. Seriously, why does it only happens after the engagement that all girls of this world start looking pretty and more beautiful than your fiancé.

At times Max would think, whether he had taken the right decision to marry Stella, was she a good enough catch. Ah, that was all good. Stella was loving, caring, and she was all he had ever wanted. Plus everybody in the family loved Stella. But seriously waiting for orders at restaurant at times gets awkward, especially when there are beautiful women sitting around you. No not Stella, of course she was beautiful, but there were more charming faces around. Finally the food came in, and they both realized that hitting a fancy restaurant always was compromising with your diet.

Max said, "Seriously, this is your version of nice food. I mean our dog poops more than this.".

Stella said, "You can thank me later, for keeping a difference in our dog and in my man.".

Max exhaled, "You know what, if all chefs of this world would be women, there won't be any hunger problem in the world. You know why. Because then hunger won't remain a problem, but a new norm.".

Stella laughed, "Ha Ha. You know what, if all the chefs of this world be men, there won't be any restaurants. You know why, because it is only the men that don't know how to cook.".

Max said, "You know what I am not paying for this food.".

Stella said, "Fine with me, even our dog doesn't pays for his food. Tell me something new.".

Max snapped back, "So why don't you marry our dog and not me.".

Stella sipped wine and said, "Honey, there is hardly any difference.".

Max sat back with grumpy face, while Stella had won the argument. She was enjoying her wine, and also the food. By the way, they had also asked the waiter on who was the chef, and it turned out it was a woman. And if woman was to be a chef, then someone, or probably Max had to stay hungry. So he was, trying to pick every last piece of salad and thin pasta with the fork. Seriously, if someone was to ask Max then the garnishing of the food was more than the food itself. His phone rang, Max wiped his hands and saw it was an unknown private number, he picked it.

The woman on call said, "Hey Max my man, how are you. It's been so long.".

Max couldn't recognize the voice and said, "No it hasn't been long but just 15 seconds.".

Woman said, "Ah your sense of humor, presence of mind and great IQ still remains unshakable. So I want you to ask something. What is it that embarrasses a man most?".

Max snapped, "For now, it will be telling my fiancé that a woman is asking me out. Not much embarrassing.".

Before Max could roast her further, the woman hung up the phone. That was strange, that the woman didn't asked Max for some charity fundraiser, or some electoral appeal, or maybe offers of buying some stocks. Yeah, Max was used to such phone calls, and had made his habit of roasting such people. This was the best way to mark off your Phone Number from such lists. Anyways now that the food was gone, Max was busy sipping the wine.

Seriously does wine even counts as food. For Max, for now, it did. Max shared a joke with Stella to which both were laughing. Meanwhile a bunch of men dressed in rugged jackets and jeans were walking towards Max from behind. One man accidently hit Max's head from behind and said, 'Watch out', while the other man swayed his hands on backless top of Stella, that was it, Max stood up trying to stop those men.

Max yelled, "Hey, you prick that is not your momma's ass, but my wives back.".

The man turned around, while Stella held Max's hand trying to calm him. "Hey Max, it's okay. He is an asshole.".

Max turned back, "Not just an ass hole, but an ass hole full of shit. What are you looking at pricks.".

Everybody in the restaurant had got their heads turned around. They were precisely four men, and each of the men was least 2 and a half times more of Max. But Max stood his ground. The man came in and stood chest to chest with Max, while the other man who had hidden a small bat in his jacket, took it out and hit hard on Max's head. Whoa what was that, Stella yelled Max's name, while all the four men started beating Max out of the blue.

Max tried resisting, but the first bat hit was too strong for Max to had regained consciousness. His head was bleeding, while these men were thumping their hardened leather boots in his chest. It hurt, and Max took the chair and thrashed it on one of the men, while he was fallen on ground. It didn't made any difference, and the men kept beating him. The waiters had called the police. One of the men gripped Max's neck and got it closer to his face.

The hoodlum said, "Hope you enjoyed it, because the game has just begun.".

The hoodlums left while Stella rushed in. Max said slowly, "Am I looking like shit.".

Stella kissed him hard on his lips, "Max, you always look like shit. But the most lovely shit ever. Come on.".

Stella lifted him on her shoulders. Wait, a woman lifting a man on her shoulders, this was the death of man code, and our Max couldn't have let that happen, so he made Stella wrap her arms around his back. Seriously it had hit hard. Max was a straight guy, wait not as in straight who always in interested in women, of course he was that kind of straight too, but in here by straight meant, a man who stayed away from wrangles, and dog fights. But guess what, a man could never stay away from wrangles, I mean at some point or other they would of course catch up with you.

But seriously, what was that, few men out of nowhere, come and mess up with them, and then beat the shit out of Max. Wait, was that some enemy from past, but Max had no enemies, he just had friends, and friends of friends. Seriously Max was never coming back to this restaurant. What cheap stake people visited this place, and this restaurant was unbelievable. I mean in past they had refused Max and Stella to enter just because the dress code wasn't right, and today these four baseball players were roaming like if it were super bowl finals. Of all, how could that man touch Stella's back, and in case if Max was to bump into them again, he would surely settle the score for not beating him up, but for touching her back, on a whole what a Saturday it was, being driven to home with bleeding hands and head, by his fiancé. On way, Stella got out to pick some bandages, antiseptics from medical store, while Max saw his wounds, god they were deep. His phone rang.

The woman said, "Now you know what embarrasses a man the most, getting beaten up by other men in front of your woman. I hope it isn't hurting much.".

Max said, "Oh thanks for the General knowledge, but I am good with masters in finance.".

The woman laughed, "Oh man, you will be grateful for what I did. They don't teach this in colleges, Max.".

Max softly said, "Of course they don't, and I am grateful that they don't.".

The woman said, "Hmm. As I clearly see you aren't able to recall to whom you are speaking with. Why not, It's been so long, and I had thought that by now you must have become a hell of a man, but I guess there is lot of work to be done. But worry not, now i am back in your life.".

Before Max could say anything else, the woman hung up the phone. Seriously, lessons of Manhood, to a man by a woman, what was it, some high adrenalin realty show. Ah, so there it was, those hoodlums didn't beat Max just because of nothing, but because of this crazy woman. But who was she. Max tried remembering hard, but couldn't recognize that voice, not even from all ones that he had made it moaned during nighty things. Wait, was this some sort of revenge, it has to be, which woman would get him beaten up bad like this. Max looked around, and felt scared for a second to see Stella standing, telling him to put down the phone and relax.

Max switched off his phone, and stretched the seat to its maximum. Max thought, should he tell Stella about this call, well she would react very badly, to know there is some woman on to him. Max avoided, like he always did when he saw a beautiful woman thinking, it would take too much efforts to work on it, well it was same with Stella at first time, but Stella coped up with his lazy efforts, and now here they were together. The road back home felt very long, seriously after a fight, everything doesn't seem to just end. They entered back in home, only to see that Jack had dropped by. Jack was Max's best friend, yeah the sort of best friend that would do all dirty things together.

Jack looked at Max and said, "Hey, hey, hey. What is that? Did you fell into a man hole?".

Max snapped back, "Seriously. Let us just take you and push into a man hole, and see if you get bruises like these.".

Jack said, "Okay, so I smell some serious business. Did you got beaten up?".

Max snapped back, "Why are you like that Jack. I got into a fight and not got beaten up.".

Stella interrupted in between, "Hey guys, I am not seeing another fight on the same night. And Jack, your friend did got beaten up, by bunch of hoodlums that came out of nowhere to mess up with us. One of them even touched my back, so Max lost his cool, and this happened.".

Jack yelled at Max, "How could he, even I haven't yet touched Stella's back.".

Max said, "Seriously, just give it a try, and maybe I will feel good for what I will do next.".

Jack said, "No Max, you don't get it, this is outrageous. Listen we are going to Police Station, right now, and file case of assault. I know a policeman in nearby station. Let us make these bastards, pay for it. I hope that was all recorded in CCTV, not because I will binge watch it, but for Police.".

Stella said, "We are inviting no more trouble. I think Jack is enough for now.".

Well Stella was right, Jack was enough for now, as both he was no less than a trouble, and two he was good enough muscle for those hoodlums. But it was not Stella who got beaten up, or rather got in a fight, it was Max whose head still had blood clots, and hands with bruises. Max couldn't have let those guys go, in fact any man would never settle especially after getting beaten up, so Max said yes to Jack and they both got headed to Police Station while the wounds were still fresh. Seriously if you got to screw a man, get Police involved in it. But in here it wasn't sure as who was screwing who, as those hoodlums were hard to catch considering their acts, and it was Max who was getting involved with Police.

They reached Police Station, and sat amidst crooked elements of the society. Seriously, Max's marriage date was coming closer, and conflicts in his life had already started worsening. Why it is that women have been source of all great wars and enemity. Yes they have been, look back in past and history. Take Helen of Troy, or Draupadi of Mahabharata, or Margaret of Anjou, and for now take Stella of Nightindale. Seriously, was Stella going to be remembered in history, who knew? Wait, but what about that woman who had called Max. He thought, whether he should mention it to Police or not. What if, there was some of Max's historic dirt involved in. This time was crucial, as his marriage was approaching and Max couldn't jeopardize it. Police Man approached.

Policeman said, "So, what is your problem.".

Jack excitedly said, "Hey he doesn't has a problem. He got beaten up, I mean he got in a fight. There are some hoodlums disturbing peace of the city, and the only problem is that they are not in jail.".

Policeman said, "I think you are in much more pain than him, are you his boyfriend.".

Jack said, "Hey, does it look like I have worn a rainbow colored tee, No. But look at his head, you see colors.".

Policeman said, "Okay, any suspects, or any identification of assaulters.".

Jack said, "Seriously, we are full grown beer drinking men. If we'd known, do you think still we'd come to you for LGBT rights of this city.".

The Policeman exhaled and got another officer to see them, while the senior officer Jason was keenly listening to their discussion, and it has piqued him on how strange it looked beaten up by some men without any reason in one of posh restaurant. The CCTV footage got in, and Policemen filed the report. Jason had also sensed that Max was hiding something. But then a call from Deputy came in and Jason went on to attend other things. Meanwhile Jack didn't stopped showing his manhood to the Police officer. He even stretched back his tee to show baby muscles that he had developed in last 2 month of hitting the gym. Both were now headed back.

Max said, "Hey Jack I also got a call from some mysterious woman, while all this happened.".

Jack snapped back, "She better stay mysterious, Max you are getting married. And that woman, wait, was her voice sexy. Ah, it has to be, or you wont be thinking about her you nasty prick. Come on give me her number and forget.".

Max exhaled, "You are not getting it. It feels she was avenging for something.".

Jack said, "Ah I get it, she must be an Iron Man fan. Do not worry I will give her some of my iron.".

Max said, "Unbelievable. Okay just do me a favor, don't tell this to Stella.".

Jack braked the car, "Don't tell me you already had phone sex with her.".

Chapter 3

When trouble comes, you get to know how strong your family and friends are. Seriously, Max had strong friends for sure, in fact as the likes of Iron man, but his family was even stronger. While Max had headed to Police Station, Stella had called Daisy and Fred. Leaving aside all the differences, Fred had driven Daisy in mid of night to their home. Thankfully neither Stella nor Daisy had told about this to rest of family, or there already been Christmas sized gathering in the house.

Max entered his home and felt sigh of relief to see her sister. Seriously, Daisy was the woman who had always been cover for Max, be it from teenage sneaking out of house in midnight, or hosting house parties for friends when parents were away, or crashing dad's car while secretly driving under age. Daisy has been the shield of excuses, a perfect sister, and tonight she looked scared. Fred had already got talking to his lawyer friend to sue the restaurant. The family had got back together on their feet.

Daisy said, "Max, you will be alright, and you did good by going to Police.".

Fred said, "Now you see Max, what I and my friends will do to these perpetrators.".

Max rose up his arms, "Hey guys, its all okay. Everything is under control. It was a bad moment and it has passed.".

Fred said, "Every bad moment of yours has to pass by us too, Max.".

Max caressed Daisy's hairs and said, "Okay, who is in for some ice cream. I hope nobody passes that.".

This was Max and his loving family, all for one, one for all. But seriously the entire night, not the whole of it, as it was meant to be slept, Max didn't spoke much to Stella, the reason was why did she called Daisy. This was Max, who always kept his problems to himself, but would never hesitate to extend an arm for family whenever needed. This was man, Stella was about to get married, and she was also excited about it. The morning came in, and everything was back to normal, including wounds of Max that had healed quite a lot. He got dressed up, ate the little toast, and whole lot of orange juice. He was back again on road to the commercial district of Nightindale, Cross Street where in a tall building his office was.

He worked with Catalyzers Inc., it was an investing and incubating firm, and Max was a venture capitalist. Yeah, this is what he always had wanted to be, a number guy. Everybody in Catalyzers knew that Max had the best eye in recognizing potential of startups. In fact, with the good reputation in the firm, his boss was thinking of making him a partner. So everything was in line for Max. He stepped into the office and got to his chamber, where few new faces waited on the couch, along with his office buddy Jeff.

Jeff said, “Hey, what is wrong with the face of this company.”.

Max exhaled, “Ah, a little liquidation, being bullish about it, and then crashing down.”.

Jeff said, “Oh I got this, you got beaten up, that too by a union.”.

Max said, “Hey, that was a fight, and I stood a great chance, but this guy cheated with an inside weapon.”.

The man sitting on couch interrupted, “Worry not sir, this is where we come in. Whenever life hits you hard, we will be always on your side. Just beside you, shoulder to shoulder.”.

Max said, “Trust me, what happened last night, you too would have fallen, if you’d be there, by my side. Presuming you haven’t shrunk while you woke up this morning. By the way, are you here to sell some security services? Because in a country like this, I can get guns in any convenience store.”.

Jeff laughed, “Hey, he is Barry. He has a startup that provides personal insurance.”.

Max sat on his chair, “Have you got yourself covered. I mean what if I just reject your pitch.”.

This was a day in Max’s life. His Business team used to work their ass off and get people like Barry visit Catalyzers in hopes of getting funded, while Max roasted all of them. In fact just like Barry, others too had thought, what is this, some kind of get insulted for free program. But it was a testing protocol of Max to test perseverance, and patience. He had other tactics too, as trusting someone you never knew before, with loads of money was worse than trusting you wife with your credit card. The risks were high, and chances very low that from that credit card spend you would get something in return for yourself.

It didn't appear for a minute that last night Max had a fight, yes he didn't got beaten up. But wait, who was that woman. Max took out his cellphone, and entered the phone number in Google, but no results came back in. He tried using some of the phone tracking websites, but still no results. This woman was strange. I mean which woman from his past would like Max to get into a fight, and yes get him beaten up. It didn't rang a bell, wait, it did rang a bell. Yes the cell phone of Max was ringing again. He picked it.

The woman said, "Max my Love. Tell me, what is it that man derives pleasure from.".

Max snapped back, "I know who you are. You are a fucking whore, you couldn't get my cock to suck. But guess what, nothing is going to change. You will have to satisfy yourself with some Chicken wings.".

The woman laughed, "Ah, here it is my man, my Max. But you didn't answered my question.".

Max said, "Oh try sending your hoodlums in my office, and they will see what company I got. By the way, there is also an insurance guy right outside. So everything is covered up.".

The woman snapped back, "Its hatred, and fulfilling that hatred.".

Max said, "I think you need to see a doctor, and when you do see him, don't suck on his stethoscope.".

The woman continued, "Listen very carefully Max. Today you are going to fire somebody that you hate most, and write him a worst relieving letter to ensure that he doesn't gets a job anywhere else. If you don't do so, I will tell the CEO that you overlooked the history documents of Alpha AI that you funded, out of personal benefits. Just do this Max, and become a Man. A true man, and do enjoy while you do it.".

The woman hung up phone. Seriously, what was it, Max thought? Was this woman mad or what. Fire somebody you hate most. Max held his head and reclined back, while Oscar entered the room. Max coughed up, as this can't be happening. Max was a true gentleman, who never hated somebody, but if you belong to planet Earth, you got to have hate in some corner of your heart, and that hate in office was reserved for Oscar. He was the sturdiest guy in Catalyzers, who would fight with anyone on pettiest of things, talk rudely, and show no respect to blue collared staff.

He came in and handed over the wrapping up documents of Alpha AI. Seriously, this woman had hands deep down in Max's throat. There do was a problem in historical accounts of this company that Max hadn't told the board just because he had a great gut feeling for this company, but how did that witch knew about it. Max told himself, ah this is some dirty prank, and will soon be over, and no one is getting fired today. World is happy place and Max will do everything to keep the world happy. He reached out to the coffee machine and started pouring himself one. Wait, what was that, a cracking sound came in from meeting room.

"You are fired. How come you not notice that this firm had outstanding debts?".

The other board member said, "Of course he noticed it, and he took bribe so we won't come to notice it.".

Boss said, "You are right. Now you are free to go and enjoy your life with that freaking bribe.".

Max thought, this couldn't be happening, it was exactly similar to his stand for Alpha AI, which means the boss would fire him too. Wait, if losing the job was only thing, Max would never do it, but he would also be stained of cheating the firm, or what if Boss sued him for fraud. Seriously, this can't be real. This woman is mad, oh my god. She is doing it. Max was sure that firing of this guy was not incidental, and that woman for sure had something to do with it. Last night he got beaten up, and now he would be fired. His marriage was only days away. He reached Jeff.

Max said, "Hey Jeff there is some woman, who is playing games with me.".

Jeff chuckled, "You want me to join in, to take her 2 down. Ha ha. Come on who is the catch.".

Max's phone rang, and it was the woman. Woman said, "You are forgetting the basic rules Max. Of course you can tell the story, but only when it is over. Getting it.".

Shit, this just got so real. Max turned around, but there were too many women he could see, some even on phone, some working on their desktop. But he knew all of them, and no one could do this to him. His eyes fell on the CCTV cameras. Shit, she is watching me. Max held his head, while Jeff kept asking him on who this woman was, and maybe Max should pass her number to him. Seriously, Jeff didn't knew that he was better off without her. This can't be happening. A woman who just had got beaten him up the other night, would not stop in seeing Max getting fired. Max thought, what should I do, wait, she had already said on what to do. But firing Oscar and ruining his career was so cruel. How could Max do something like that to his colleague. But then what would happen of family, that has tried so hard to stand on their feet and made society respect them. Everything will be gone in seconds.

Max threw the cup of coffee, and went inside his cabin to drink chilled water. Max told himself, okay I have to do this. There is no way out. Shit, why did he funded Alpha AI, those men were no brothers to him. Max took a deep breath, and called Oscar to see him in the office in 15 minutes. Hell no, he thought to himself, on what he was about to do. No matter how hard Oscar was, his life will get shattered. But then it was his life versus Oscar's life. Seriously, I am not God, nor I am an angel to Oscar, and this venture has to go this way. Plus Oscar was no good to anyone in this office, maybe that wretched woman was making Max do something good after all. Max opened his laptop and made his mind shut all the thoughts. Oscar entered the room.

Max said, “Hey sit down Oscar. You must have had a good day. But please know that nothing is permanent. So I am just going to rip that good from your day and make it like just another day.”

Oscar interrupted, “Oh worry not, a day with you can never be good. Tell me what I need to do.”.

Max said, “Oh that’s great, because you no longer have to bear me, and there is nothing for you to do.”.

Oscar flickered, “Wait a minute. Am I being transferred, because I’ve already filed an application for stay.”.

Max said, “I wish it were that simple to stay. But you are being fired.”.

Max handed the worst relieving letter he had ever written, even seen, ever heard of. Seriously, he had put in every thing he hated about Oscar, seriously everything that would ward off any future employer. The letter went like this. ‘To whom so ever it concerns, blah, blah, and then coming to the point. I wish I had got the chance to thank you for your service, and your time. But you never served me well, all you did was serve time as convicts do in jail. Seriously, our office might have four walls around it, but then it doesn’t means it is a jail, because we have lot many windows too and a balcony from where all you did was hanging on to your cup of coffee and cigarettes while your time in here. Your knowledge about Investing is zero, which I should have realized when you called this place a catholic bank. I thought it was a joke, but then you went to crucify a colleague of yours in a dirty fight. This we can never forget, especially Justin who every week waits for his Good Friday so he won’t have to see your face for another two days. You are the rudest person I have ever came across, and our janitor agrees with it too, who pays special attention to clean your cubicle in hopes that your life becomes dirt free and someday you be thankful to him for keeping the place clean. To top everything, last summer you really showed who you really are, a Racist, by throwing that plate of noodles on our Chinese Colleague pretending it was a mistake, but asking him later that you must have enjoyed the taste. With all these extraordinary abilities, attitude and intellect, we no longer can bear you. If you think this is all normal in life, try taking another job with this letter.'. While Oscar read it, he couldn't believe himself, in fact if Max was to read it again, he wouldn't believe on how he had been tolerating Oscar for so long. Oscar blew up instantly by throwing a little heap of files on Max's table. He strode out of cabin to working floor.

Oscar yelled, "This is bigotry. Just because i can't pretend to be a nice man, doesn't means I am not nice.".

Max saw this coming, and said from behind, "We are just firing you, not putting you on fire. Stop it.".

Oscar yelled back, "I will not. Everybody knows that you hate me. I will take it to the boss.".

Max calmly said, "Me. Come on, everybody hates you, even the boss. Go try him.".

Oscar didn't stopped and showed the letter to few of the people that showed little sympathy in the moment, but seriously Oscar do was most hated man of this company. Jeff came close by to Max, and patted on his back with a chivalry smile. The boss of Catalyzers, Bruce too came in hearing all loud voices. The floor of Catalyzers had went upside down, and few of young Start up owners were feeling little scared seeing Oscar take charge of revolt.

Bruce said, "Calm down Oscar, this happens with everyone. You are not the only one.".

Oscar snapped back, "Seriously, because it is just me who is getting fired."

Bruce said, "Oh no, you don't get my point. I mean, everyone has to leave the company, one day or the other. It is cycle of life, and if Max thinks you are unfit, then you got to take your laundry away with you.".

Oscar turned back to Max, "This isn't done Max. You think you are the man, you'll regret it.".

Hey, hey, hey, what you said, what was Max wanted to reply back, but seriously he couldn't, it was guilt that stopped him. Oscar rashly went on his desk, and was already on his way out. Max thought, this was not right, or maybe it was. He could see smile on that Chinese Colleague, and a huh on face of Janitor.

Wait, did he said, you think you are a man, no way Oscar was somebody associated with that woman. Seriously two days, and Max had started doubting if he was even a man, or he should think that he was becoming a man. Did he got pleasure from this hatred, a little bit, as Oscar do was a scum in Catalyzers. This woman was insane, but one thing was sure that she knew everything about Max, including Oscar.

This was definitely not a good day, neither for Max, nor for Oscar. But still Max was in doubt and little fear, if that woman would still not disclose the Alpha AI funding shortcomings to Bruce. He waited for a couple of hours, avoided everybody and would drop by Bruce's chamber every 15 minutes making one or other excuse. He even tried calling back on the same number that woman had used, but all he heard was that please check the number you have dialed. Maybe she was gone. But seriously wasn't her ways strange to make Max a man. Wait I mean Max was already a man, only if that woman had some different definition of manhood. God, he thought, his mother would be so upset to hear that Max did such a thing. It was last hours of the office and Jeff came in.

Jeff said, "Here you are. Here is my man. Thanks for relieving us of Oscar.".

Max exhaled, "Oh so before this I wasn't man. And also know that there are lot of Oscars in this world, so many that chances of new recruit replacing him of being the same are 50:50.".

Jeff frowned, "I worry no more, because amidst all these 50 Oscars, we have 1 Max.".

Jeff continued, "And wait, who said you weren't a man before. You were always my man.".

Max held his head, "You know, this all firing of Oscar, somebody made me do it, the same woman who got me beaten up last night. She is crazy and comes out of nowhere. She thinks she is trying to make me a man. And also you are right, there is only 1 Max, and I am glad that he is like he is.".

Jeff laughed, "True. But wait, is that the same woman whose number I was asking for.".

Max engrossedly said, “Yeah, and it’s the number all that I have, that too appears to be wrong when I dial back.”.

Jeff snapped back, “Oh I get it, you know what Max you can keep the number as I pass to this woman, and I am not telling Stella a thing about it. Come on, you aren’t married yet. Take this woman to some nice hotel and show her that yeah babe you have made me a man grrr. And listen, tonight, we are going to hit the club, all of the catalyzers. In fact we are celebrating Oscar’s firing. Ain’t this cool, so meet me at the parking.”.

Chapter 4

Seriously an office party on someone getting fired. This has to be the first one, and one of its kind. Max couldn't say a no, after all he was the hero of the party, how could he be not there. But if someone was to ask Max, he didn't felt even a bit good about this party, about this day, about this woman. Max could simply not stop thinking about these last two days, and that strange woman. This was the most bizarre thing that had ever happened to him, someone trying to make him a man. In fact for minute she made him believe that he did enjoyed firing Oscar. Did really men enjoyed hatred, well Max could never know because asking such question would raise another set of questions. But Jeff really thought it was cool, and so did the other people in his office.

They entered a nearby club, and all Max could see was women standing in corner, alone, in groups, gossiping, and all Max could think was, whether the same woman was here too watching him. No way, her work was done, though her number was out of service. Max went straight to the bar table and got himself a shot of vodka. A woman passed by swaying her hands on Max's back. He immediately turned around and saw her giving a flying kiss. Was that her, no she looked too sexy to get herself in such smudgy business. Ah, maybe Max should let it go, and let her go from his thoughts, for his family and Stella waiting back at home. Max joined his colleagues in shaking some legs on the floor. They went back to another table and ordered some food, while that Chinese guy, Chang came in towards Max.

Chang said, "You have no idea Max, how much we hated Oscar, all of us. You did good."

Max said, "Tell me one thing, that did you really liked the taste of noodles that Oscar threw on you that day.".

Jeff interrupted, "Hey Max, whose side you are on. Hey don't mind him, he is just having a not so great day. You know how does it feels after firing another man, and of course he knows you didn't liked the noodles that day. I think he is joking, Right Max. You know he is just overwhelmed. We will see you in a minute.".

Jeff turned to Max, "Seriously, all you thought about was noodles, as you have ordered them too. Now eat this Chinese shit. Wait, I hope Chang is gone, because I can't turn around, having said that.".

Max said, "Yeah he is gone, so has Oscar, and so has that woman.".

Jeff turned around to see Chang go and turned back to Max, "Seriously, we are trying to have some good time here, and all you can think is about that woman. You know what, I will leave you with that woman, so just figure out, how big her butts would be, or the color of her hair, or shade of her lipstick, but I am going.".

Max got himself another shot of vodka, while he sat alone on the bar table. His phone rang. Holy Hell, it was the woman. Max turned his eyes to gaze every other woman in club, but couldn't find even one worth the suspect. She was still watching Max, and probably this wasn't over. Max didn't answered the phone. But there she was again calling him. Max gulped his drink and picked the phone.

The woman said, "See Max, it is that simple to be a man. Now your entire office knows who the man is.".

Max snapped back, "The man that entire office knows, wants to know, that who is this woman."

Max continued, "And yes being a man is simple, which simply you don't get.".

The woman said, "Max don't strain yourself, because I have just got started. Okay you take your time, enjoy this manly moment of yours, have couple of more shots, till my next question. And trust me, you are going to love the rest of your life, on what I am going to do next.".

The woman hanged up. Seriously, what was happening in Max's life, what was this, this ugly game of becoming this woman's version of man. Enjoy, did she really think after hearing that she would be back, Max would enjoy. This was not over, in fact she had just got started. What did this woman want, in a world where nobody does nothing without any reason. Jeff came back in trying to drag Max on the club dancing floor, but Max refused in the most manly way, and to that the other office member cheered. Seriously, where these people too thinking that this how men do it.

The voice of the woman just echoed in Max's head, while he drove back home. He hadn't heard that voice ever, and even if he did, he didn't remembered, because being a man, okay being somebody already engaged to love of his life, it was not required to remember voices of other woman. This wretched woman had already made Max fire someone, now what did she else wanted Max to do, because she was for sure not going to get Max beaten up, as that was first question. Max was tired and straightaway went for bed without even saying a hello to Stella, who had sensed that something was wrong. She sneaked in under the blanket to cover Max with her arms.

Stella said, "You know I was thinking what if Brooce Willis was a venture capitalist. He would surely pick up truck pickup companies for one, he would invest in alcoholic firms whenever market crashes down, he would break bonds that don't work, ah even the James Bond. In all he would do well. Then I thought what if I were to marry someone like Brooce. I mean he would take me to highway diners, and yes never get beaten up in front of me. Hhhhhaha.".

Max interrupted, "And he would also break the bed every time you'd get naughty.".

Stella stopped his hands, "This is not what I meant. Let's go to that, ah, 'Men are back' tomorrow.".

Max said, "But still nice to have my woman back in my arms.".

Stella slept within minutes the light went off, but Max still couldn't stop thinking about whatever was happening in his life. No way, he was going to tell Stella, and ring trouble on her head. But something needed to be done about this woman. Max was both scared, and expecting the next call anytime soon. The entire night he kept looking at his phone, which was kept on the bedside table. The entire night he couldn't sleep more than 15 minutes in a row. Morning crept in, and it was as usual for Stella, but for Max something else was going to happen, what it could be, he couldn't stop thinking. Max ate more than usual breakfast, as he knew that this day was going to be a long one. He got on to his car and another car passed by with two women looking straight in his eyes.

Max reached his office, and couldn't stop seeing the faces of his colleagues thinking if he had to fire another one. Max was completely absent minded, he even rejected couple of startups he had been nurturing for final pitch to boss. He was loosing it, and it was evident that Max's life was no more the same. Today he didn't took even a single break to have coffee with Jeff, he didn't used the washroom even once, he didn't even had his lunch in the cafeteria, he was busy looking at his Facebook profile trying to find every woman he was connected with, he was busy checking every other email contact which was female, and nothing occurred to him, I mean who could do this to him. Max left the office early, and as promised he picked Stella and they went on to see 'Men are back'. The theatre was half empty and they had taken corner seat, while the entire time Max rested his forehead on his palms.

In movie Brooce Willis said, "You don't know what it takes to be a man. If it were only about balls, every soccer players would be a Super Man.".

Another character said, "Yeah, that is why we only have one Babe Ruth.".

Brooce Willis turned around, "And one Brooce who is now going to batter your balls.".

The villain said, "You are not getting it, you can batter, you can hit, but these balls will always be out of your reach.".

Then girlfriend of Villain double crosses him by pointing gun on his balls, "Trust me, they are no good.".

In all of this Max couldn't help but smile, not because of the movie. Yes, inspite of Brooce Willis being his favorite, today he was not engrossed in the movie, but in the fact that Stella just for him to cheer up was pretending very hard to concentrate watching the movie and enjoying it too. Seriously, if God was there, he must have been very happy with Max for sending this woman in his life. For the rest of the movie, Max simply rested his head on her shoulders, and pretended to be a man who would deal with any kind of man shit. They reached home, but still Max couldn't get over the fact that something again was going to happen, and after having spent time with Stella, he was now more scared if that woman didn't involved Stella in her dirty games.

I mean that woman could do anything. She had already hurt Max, once, but wait, back in restaurant, she didn't involved Stella, though she was right there. Ah, what had Max done in past to have pissed off this woman. He couldn't remember a thing. Max went on to his office, and as usual met some of the startup founders, but today he didn't roasted any one of them, while Jeff was little surprised to see Max not so in mood. He confronted Max.

Jeff said, "Hey, what's wrong with you. Are you missing Oscar's blowjobs? I mean his blowing up every job.".

Max calmly said, "Seriously, is that why you wanted him out of my life, what you want some now.".

Jeff said, "That is how my man rolls. Yeah, I mean not how you roll on me, as you never have, but just lit up, I know something is troubling you, but just keep blowing it, you know. Okay i am right there on floor.".

Max's phone rang, and it was the woman. Max closed the doors of his cabin, and blocked the window curtains. He kept his phone on the table, and bit his hands. Seriously, he had never wanted this woman to call again, but at the same time he had also hoped to all of this be over as soon as possible. God, but these two things were so different, and so was the thinking of Max and this woman. Seriously, one more question to be a man. Max picked it.

The woman, "Hey Max, this one is simple. What makes a man a man?".

Max said, "Wait, there can't be two kind of men, and I am not that kind of man.".

The woman laughed, "Okay I will make it simple, What is the source of manhood?".

Max snapped back, "Here it is on your tongue. You can have it, it won't get dirty. Feeling any surprised.".

The woman laughed, “You got it right, finally you are getting to know me. But i have nothing to with your cock, you can keep it. But to make you a man, you got to do something with it. Circumcision it is, surprise, and yes you got to do this, if you want to save your father. You will get to know soon that it is only me, who can now save your father. Time to bid adieu to your cock’s cover.”.

The woman hanged the phone. Wait, that was not at all happening anytime soon. Did she just said, Circumcision, like peeling off the skin of his cock. She was totally out of her head. I mean how could Max do that, was this some sick joke. This woman had gone crazy. I mean what woman would want another man’s circumcision. Wait, she said, if I wanted to save my father. As far as Max remembered it was last night he had spoken with his father. What a joke, and then Max’s eyes fell on the phone. Ah, if anything bad, god forbid might have happened to his father, he would be the first one to know. Max remembered the policeman friend of Jack, and he made his mind to report this phone call to Police, maybe then she would know how Police – MEN are. This game was so over. Max’s phone rang.

Daisy said, “Max, dad is in hospital, I don’t know what to do. Doctors are giving up.”.

Max was shaken, “Hey, hey, hey. Do not worry, where are you? And know that, we might not be a doctor, nor are we are giving up on dad.”.

This crazy woman was about to die by hands of Max, as he thought, and all he could think was a blurred face with neck in tight grips of Max’s hands. Seriously, what had dad done with her, to get him dragged in this become a man game. Max knew that this woman must have ensured that there was only one way of saving dad, and that was listening to her and getting circumcised. God, Max was neither Islamic nor a Jew, and of all he was proud of how his genitals had kept him gentle. But first he had to see his dad who was admitted in Cross Line Hospital. Max reached, and his entire family had gathered in the lobby of hospital. They hugged Max, while the only person not around his arms was Fred who was busy on phone. Seriously, there was no remedy to the illness Fred had. Most probably he must have been talking to his friends to find the best doctors in town.

Daisy started crying, while Stella tried to kept her calm. Max's father, Charles had a liver problem from quite a past, and he has been on medicinal treatment from quite long. But today something had triggered it, and his liver had just stopped working. The only way to save him was a liver transplant, that too within a day or two. Good news was that organ donors were everywhere, but the bad news was that there was a huge waiting list for them, and the next liver was going to be available in another 3 months. Charles didn't had that much of time. So in a nutshell, he was about to die, unless a donor came in forward to volunteer. Everybody in Max's family was feeling helpless, while deep in his heart Max knew that this entire situation was in its place because of him. Now it was Max's responsibility to get things right, continue playing her game, and make his dad fit for approaching Thanksgiving dinner.

Daisy said, "I don't know what happened. He was at our house playing with Esther, then he collapsed.".

Max's younger brother Jose said, "It's the first time, and doctors say it will be the last.".

Max snapped back, "Hell with them. He wasn't playing with Esther. He is playing with all of us. You know he is peeping through those eyes and watching us. So we got to be strong. Okay."

Fred came in, "Ah, there are chances that one of my friend can arrange liver from black market.".

Max said, "Seriously, and what will he do with it when police will take him and us to jail. And you know what, this black market liver will not be able to digest any liquor which dad likes, which isn't available in jail. Oh wait, your friends will sure be able to smuggle some in.".

Fred interrupted, "Oh, you have a better idea, please share, because anyway you can't share your liver.".

Daisy stepped in between, "Stop it Max, and Fred. You can fight when he is gone, but not now.".

Max said, “Oh yes he is going, but you know where, to Europe.”.

Everyone had eyes fixed on Max, thinking what was he saying, I mean what was he doing. The idea behind it was, that Max had a college friend Arthur, who was now working with Doctor’s Association of Europe. Yes he was a high ranking official in the association, and a very close friend of Max too. Once when he was back in his hometown during a college reunion, he had told Max that lots of Rich patients who didn’t got organs in their home country, searched for donors in Europe, or search for volunteer donors, and many a times they got it too. Now Arthur had access to all the databases of donors, so he could have helped now. Max was not very rich though, but he had saved enough money to buy back life of his father. Seriously, Max didn’t even had many friends too, but Arthur somehow was one of them few.

Max called him, and told everything about the situation of his father. While Max did so, he was getting positive response from Arthur, and Max couldn’t stop smiling to his fate that he would no longer have to listen to that wretched woman, because Max was as good a man to save his father.

Arthur said, “Ah, all looks good. We have 2 donors in Belarus that are available, and 1 in Ukraine.”.

Max said, “I don’t know where these places are, but you are right now in my heart.”.

Arthur said, “Hey wait. Most important thing, is he okay to travel in a flight.”.

Max turned, while all were listening closely and Fred came forward to pat his back. “You know Max, he is not only your father, but mine too, and Daisy’s too. We have already tried.”.

Life was unfair, and life always bit on your back whenever you wanted most to sit down and have the moment of life. This close, to see his father to be okay, but doctors had already said that air travel was fatal for Charles. And now Max had no one to call to, he didn’t had friends with connection in black market, and neither was he making Fred take such a risk which was a federal offence. God, what would he do now, circumcision, of course, that was it. Anyways it was just his cock and it would do same good as without its skin. Max's phone rang.

The woman said, "Didn't knew about Arthur. For a minute, I completely lost it to you.".

Max said, "Hey, I will do what you say. But I just want my dad back.".

Chapter 5

The woman smiled and Max could it see it through, "He is yours, all yours. Just calm down, and listen. Go to the parking, get in your car, go back home, enter the bathroom, shut off the lights, open your pants, and just cut that freaking piece of flesh of your cock. And a donor who is waiting for my nod will appear up in hospital. And Max, trust me you are the only man in your family, who can save Charles.".

Max said, "Oh Thanks for the manual, or i would be trying it in my bedroom. Just keep your donor ready.".

Max told Fred to not do anything stupid, and he will be back in couple of hours, as he was going to meet another doctor friend of his. Seriously, this woman was no ordinary, she had known everything about Max, to whom he was speaking to, to whom he was meeting, to whom he had known, and now she also had a donor, of which entire network of country's doctors didn't knew about. Okay, if it was all about getting circumcised, then be it. He got in his car, broke couple of traffic rules to reach as fast he could to his home. He exactly went into the bathroom, but didn't shut the lights. His pants were off, so were his undies, and he stood there naked, watching reflection of his cock in mirror. Max wasn't sure, but if that woman had told him to cut his entire cock, he would have considered that too for his father. He searched and got his hands on a nail cutter. Yeah, it was just about good to get rid of some flesh. Max held his cock and deliberately tried cutting it. His hands were shivering, and he was feeling very weak.

Max yelled, "Ah, that is not done, how can a man put a cut on his own cock."

He held the nail cutter and slowly tried getting rid of external layer. His hands were shivering and eyes were on verge of getting closed. He couldn't do it. He then took the file of that nail cutter to trim the skin. It hurt, and he stopped as blood started clotting up. He couldn't do it any further. HE reached out for his body deodorant and sprayed it all over his cock. Hell it hurts. It wasn't working, Max had to get himself circumcised. He took his shaving blade to use it to cut the flesh. He swiped it over the skin, and his hands left the blade in reflux. His body was not helping even a bit. Max had never felt that weak. Max's phone rang.

Woman laughed, "I knew, you would do exactly as I said. But it isn't working right.".

Max said, "Of course, only if you had tried clipping of your nipples, you'd known.".

Woman said, "Ah Max, I don't need to, because I am already a woman without doing so. Let me help you. Go see a doctor and get yourself circumcised, as you can't become a man on your own. Just kidding, but do listen to this one. And yes, when its done, click a picture of your new dick and post it on social media, with a caption telling the world, that hey, here, I am the man. And this I am not kidding about.".

Woman hanged up and Max felt so played and so stupid that he was trying to circumcise himself in his bathroom with a nail cutter and a deodorant spray. Seriously all his life he was told that good men go to Heaven, but what did he had done to deserve a living hell. This was getting insane. I mean getting circumcised was not a big deal, but his father in Hospital for that, do sure was. He knew exactly where he had to be. Max got back in his car, and went straight back to the same Cross Line Hospital. Hiding his face, he straight reached to a general surgeon who was busy with a patient. There he was, the man who was about to make him a man, as per that woman. Max took hands of doctor, stood him up, and unzipped his pants, and got laid on the bench in his cabin,

Max said, "Doc you are circumcising me right now, or this thing will be no good to you.".

Getting circumcised in your twenties was the last thing a man would want, but another last thing he would want was his dad leaving him behind. A bit of anesthesia, and closing eyes helped a lot. Before Max would knew his flesh was off the cock. It was done, but had he become a man, who would tell that, as if Max were to ask there was no difference as he felt, only that he was now more uncomfortable, and it would take least a week or so to get adjusted with this new change. Wait, the people were to tell that, as Max had to share the picture of his new cock on social media. Seriously, this woman was now becoming a pain in Max's back. If he had shared this picture, everybody would think Max was crazy, and there was family, friends and everyone on his social media accounts.

Seriously a scoop like that would also get picked by online blogs and newspapers. God, now how do I do that. Max remembered his father, and took a click of his cock. But his hands were not co operating with his mind to share it. Max could feel, that if he would take another couple of minutes, that woman would call again and tell him something new. He closed his eyes, and pushed the button post it. He rushed back towards the ward where his father was, and everyone had smile on their faces. They were happy to see Max, as if he was just the man who had did it.

Daisy said, "Dad is safe. We got a donor. Did you do anything?".

Max sighed, "I mean what could I do, in hospitals everything is done by docs, right."

Fred came in forward with a frowned face, "He is right, just check this out, where your brother has been in past one hour. He is the man, as he says with a picture, as if we have got our things shipped from Amazone.".

It started with a notification received by Fred who was as usual, quite active on his phone, and now the entire family was taking a look at Max's cock. This was the worst time it could have been, but it had to be now. Max had thought that he would explain in future to everyone why he did this, but for now his family was so upset. Doctors had said that they had to wait for another night and maybe a morning too, before the transplant took place and his dad be back in home. Meanwhile from Daisy to Stella, to Jose and other family members, Max had become a heartless prick. Max had become a man who was getting his cock worked out while his father was battling with life. It was the most insensitive thing to do, by all means. It was what a mad man would do. Posting it on social media had made Max look that he didn't even cared about Charles.

The woman had succeeded in parting Max's family from him, or why should she had asked such a thing. It was not just this, Max's phone was flooded with calls, with people asking if he was okay, and why had he posted such a thing on social media. Everyone was confused, disgusted, surprised, and lot many emotions, but Max stayed silent for a while. Should he have told them about this woman, or not, as getting family into trouble was last thing Max ever wanted. But this was not getting well anytime soon.

Max broke up, "Okay guys, there is a woman who is making me do all these things. In fact I doubt that dad fighting inside with his life is also the courtesy of this woman.".

Stella came up, "I knew it, there was some other woman, and what else she is making you do.".

Max exhaled, "Honey, you are not getting it. She is a crook. She made me fire my junior, ask Jeff.".

Stella snapped back, "No, no, no, I am getting it. She can make you do anything, and I assume the next thing will be breaking up with me, breaking our marriage, and poor Max would have no defense.".

Daisy said, "Hey Max, you can't have another woman in your life. This is not how our family is, and if you are in some trouble, then we should be the first people to know it, not some random person from Facepad.".

Fred interrupted, "Be clear Daisy, which family you are talking about, this right here, or behind the scenes one.".

Max had no option but to tell the entire story. Fred had never listened to him that carefully. Max showed them the numbers she had used to call him, but even Fred's friends couldn't find any trace of these numbers. This was it, but the most shocked person in the room was Stella. For a minute she thought , that she was about to make Max her life partner, who even for a minute didn't considered important to tell her that hey I am in some trouble and I need you. This was not how Stella had imagined her hubby to be. Had she waited her entire youth to be with someone who would do anything another woman told him to. Stella understood that this woman was blackmailing him, but would she stop, and for sure Max must have done something really bad to this woman that had made her do this.

Every one was asking Max, on whom had he screwed up in past, but Max had no answer. In fact, Stella had doubted if Max was even telling the truth. Fred was in angst that Max never considered him as a friend, or even a brother though in law. Max's family was tonight getting broken into parts, with doubts amongst them. Daisy had known that Max had never been very sweet to girls right from start, maybe this woman was one of them. After a long the entire family dined in the canteen of hospital, but tonight they all had silence on their lips. If Max was right, then this woman had just tried killing their father. Twice Fred had held Max's hand to take him to a Italian family that had huge street muscle power, but Max refused only thinking that Daisy's husband should stay away from this. This woman was after Max, and she would only get to have Max and no one else. It was almost mid night, Stella came closer to Max.

Stella said, "You know Max, I always had fantasies on how my man would be. Will he always hold my hand, will he always stay close to me, will he always protect me, will he pamper me when I be sick, but as I grew up, I came to know that each man is only for his own, and you are no exception Max.".

Max interrupted, "It's not like that Stella. Away from fairies there is war going on, always.".

Stella said, "And I want you to win, or will I look good with a loser.".

Stella placed her fingers on his lips, "It's okay Max. I don't know who this woman is, or what is she going to do next. But what I know is, that you will not let her win on us. I wish I could be a team with you on this, but I know you are too man for that. So I am calling off this wedding, for a while. Deal with her, make her taste some bronze, do everything that it takes for family, and you will find me right here, ah not in this hospital.".

Doctors had said that Charles was as good as ever again. The woman had kept her word, the only thing Max felt good about all this becoming a man. But seriously, now this woman was going nowhere until she had it back from Max. Yes, now it was Max's turn, until she rang up again, which Max was very sure that she would, because this had just felt to be getting started.

Max left the hospital to his favorite lounge where he had called both Jack and Jeff, his two of closest friends. If that woman can plan, and make Max do these dirty things, then Max too was a medal holder from University. Catching her, finding her, was now looking distant, but always in sight, till she was around. Max had told them about his condition and circumcision. Three of them sat there with no clues on where to start.

Jack said, “Max you are trying to find this woman, for revenge, or all this to stop.”.

Max looked back, “Both, or why else would I have called you two.”.

Jeff said, “Max, you don’t remember her voice, she calls every time with a new satellite number. She has no name. You don’t know what perfume she puts on, you don’t know if she wears a heel or not. In our very own Nightindale there are millions of women. I mean I love to chase women, but here the odds beat us.”

Max said, “Hey I am not a lottery winner, that woman and I have a past. This is where we start.”.

Jeff said, “Come on Max, we are not dropped by some alien ship tonight. WE too have a past.”.

Max sighed, “Seriously, and I thought you both will help. That woman and I have a past as in together, and unfortunately there are no history books on me to make it simple.”.

Jack said, “That’s it, let’s play by the books. I know a man.”.

Yes it had to get there, by the books Jack had meant, what would a man do when some mysterious woman was making him do dirty things. Hire a detective. Of course Police would also have been help, but considering that Max had already fired Oscar on conflicting grounds, Jack and Jeff had both suggested Max to not go the police. So there it was a Private Detective, and his name was Jay Aka J. Jay was an ex-policeman who has had an extremely successful career but just because of a mobster who trapped him in a bribery case, J lost his job, and here he was running a private detective agency. J had an extremely keen eye, and a great reputation of finding woman, mostly in form of alleged lovers, and in here too Max had to find a woman. Everything fit well.

Jack, Jeff and Max visited J's office, and all they could see on the soft board was explicit images of making out, kissing, lap dances etc, etc. Max felt, if he was really in the right place, but then he went on to see another rack full of Police Awards, gallantry awards, etc, etc. Well not such a bad place was it either. Now finding that woman meant Max had to spill out all his secrets, including ones he had hidden from Jack and Jeff too.

Jay said, "Max you are so screwed. I know these types of women. She must be probably single, with no signs of seeing somebody in near future. She has lots of stash left behind by her dead husband, or maybe dead father. She is upset with you, and won't stop till she turns your life upside down.".

Max said, "Hasn't she already. Right now my marriage is hanging on in a void.".

Jack said, "He is right Jay. Right now his man thing is also hanging in void. Just saying.".

Jay said, "Hey, let's not get there. Hey Max write me down all woman in your life from past, present, future.".

Jack interrupted, "Hey, he is a venture capitalist, not a tarot card reader. I mean future.".

Jay said, "That was quick. Wait, only 11. Now don't tell me, they are your wife, mother, sister, and cousins. Max listen, the first rule of investigating is trusting no one. This woman can be anyone, so think hard, take your time, and write every single woman you have known, including ones that might have just given you a boner. Trust me, its going to cost more, but you will prefer paying me, than to your past.".

Seriously all woman including ones that have given him a boner, god the list would never end then. Max got thinking from right he was born. He couldn't recall everything, but childhood stories told by Daisy flashed in his head. Remembering adult friends was not that difficult, then there were colleagues, some professional friends, some neighbors, and the list went on. An hour had passed and Max handed J a list of some 70 women.

Jay said, “This is okay for now. But take this. Once this is all over, try to work on these numbers. I mean number of women in your life. More the number, more happiness, just saying.”.

Jack interrupted, “Oh seriously, why don’t you say, more the no. more the chances of coming back to J.”.

Jay said, “Max, as per your side of story. It seems that this woman has a grudge, and it is from some deep past. So tell me, which of these woman you have hurt the most. I mean which woman felt hurt the most by you.”.

Max said, “Hey, first I don’t hurt woman. I mean I even follow sex postures from Buddha doctrine.”.

Jeff said, “Seriously. Leave Buddha out of it. He never had sex, it must be Kamasutra.”.

Max said, “It must be Nina. She was with me in school. She always had a crush on me, but we never went along like couples, because I was simply not into her. And by the time we were in High School, she held up serious grudge against me. But, she was a very quiet girl, and would not grow up to woman like this”.

Nina it was, and by the way she lived in the neighborhood just by the side of his parental house. All of them got loaded in car and they went straight to Nina’s house. Last time Max had checked, Nina had just graduated from a nearby community college. This was all he knew about her as of now. They reached her house, while J went on to ring the bell. A young woman came out and seeing nobody went inside. Max confirmed that she was Nina. Next thing, J opened his laptop to enter her name in a software he had that would give phone numbers of every person in city by a particular name. They found a match. J made a call.

J said, “Hi Nina. This is Jon from city council. We have received a complaint against you. Can you please confirm where were you last day. It is just going to help you and me.”.

Nina said, “That’s strange, because yesterday I was on patrol. You know I’m in Police. Did some thug raised this.”

J hung up the phone, and the next thing was that he drove out of the street to be as away from her home. Max smiled, not because of seeing a fellow man do a stupid thing but he was happy that Nina had made something good out of her life. She was in Police, and Max was sure that if even now he dropped by her house, she would help him, she would help her first crush. But nah, Max was not taking her help, but then now one name was almost crossed off the list, though J said that he would find some other way of tracking Nina, despite of her being in Police.

Chapter 6

The other means of finding this woman was the donor who had saved Charles's life. I mean seriously that man had waited for a nod by that woman, and for sure he must have known something about her. Max had tried his level best to get donor's details, but it was hospital policy to not let them out. Hence J had to come in, and use a little under table bribe to Hospital clerks. Finally they got the details. There it was. It was a man who had just died, and had mentioned in his organ donation will that this organ be gone to Life Care Charity, the same NGO which was contacted by Max and his family for organs, in lieu of donation. The address was of old district, and clearly this man had done it for money, as it all appeared. J had found that nobody in his closest family was an organ donor. This man just had one son who was an alcoholic, and one daughter in law who was a nurse in old districts govt. hospital.

It made sense, maybe her daughter in law had arranged for all this organ deal for some hefty money. More over this man was living on ventilator for past 2 weeks and it was on that day he got removed and died. J and Max reached his house, which was not in very good shape. His son, Leo came by.

Jay said, "Hey Leo. I know your father died, just to bring Max's father back in life. I don't mind if you made some money out of it. I mean if your dying father can bring life to some family, it is the best charity one can do. Your father was great man. All I want to know is, what woman made you do this.".

Leo said, "What do you mean by what woman. My woman of course.".

Leo's wife Luna came by, "Hey, I am that woman. And this time you ain't getting shit. Wasn't liver enough.".

Max handed over a bundle of 100 dollars, "You know what woman I am talking about, and this isn't shit.".

They got inside, but what all they got was another phone call conversation. This woman was way smart, she had contact Luna in the same fashion as she had done with Max. Luna was paid 30 K dollars for this liver, from some off shore account. All

Luna remembered about her was her dark luscious voice that she would for sure recognize once she heard again. One thing was sure that this woman was mad. I mean who would pay 30 K dollars to save father of a man whom she wants to screw that badly. But only a mad a woman, yep that was right. This lead turned out to be a dead end, and there was nothing they could do or find. Plus now it was sure that this all was planned.

The next thing J wanted to know was some woman with whom Max had an affair with but had left her for any reason leaving her being mad at him. As per Max, there was only such one woman, and she was Anna, from his college days. The fun thing was that Anna too was living in Nightindale as of now, as he had heard from few of his common friends. Such woman might not love you deeply, but they will always feel cheated, that was one, and they would never forgive you for invading their hearts, that was two, and three was that Anna knew too much about Max, so J and Max went on to hit her office. By the way she worked in a legal firm as an advisor. Meanwhile J had already seen the message received by Luna on her Mobile of payment that came from Bank of Isles with account ending with 471. He made a call to Anna, while he sat in the lobby keeping an eye on her, just to see her expressions.

Jay said, "Hey Anna, this is Jon. I am calling from Bank of Isles, and this call is in regard to your account ending with 471. You recently have made a transaction of 30 K to a new user. We just wanted to confirm if that was you.".

Anna said, "Yeah, you are right, I want my money. It wasn't me.".

As Jay looked Anna appeared very casual, and this was sure a sign that she did had an account in that bank. Jay continued, "Great Anna, so you confirm that you didn't paid that money to Luna.".

Anna said, "Of course. I didn't paid her that money, by the way who is Luna, and where is this bank of Isles.".

Jay hanged the phone and returned back to Max, with a disapproving face. But there was something fishy about Anna, which Jay was soon going to find out. Seriously, another suspect that too went in vain, this was again a failure. But in a case like this the best possibility was that this woman should have been a lover of Max who wanted a revenge for maybe being dumped. But things weren't turning out like expected. Now Jay wanted to know, if Max had any rivalry with some woman or some family dominated by a woman, or if not him, then maybe his family had some enemy. What Jay meant was, any enemy who could do this, and was a woman. Seriously an enemy woman was the last thing a man would keep, and Max was no exception. But there indeed was one woman who could do this. There was one family that hated Max's family. It was the Smith's family.

Max's family wasn't originally from Nightindale, they were immigrants to this beautiful country. When they had set foot on this land, it was Smith's family that gave them employment and a house on rent. Over the time they got very well together, but then Govt. came in between. I mean they made an announcement that immigrants living in rented homes for over 25 years will no more be tenants and be the rightful owner of that place. Max's grandfather and the other immigrant tenants took use of it and claimed over 7 houses of Smith's family. With this all Smith family came to ground and held grudge against Max's family. Today, they lived just few houses away from Max's parental home, while the lady of house Nova always saw Max and his family as thieves. This was enough for Jay, and they drove just opposite to Nova's house, which was still the biggest one in neighborhood as if, of a landlord.

Jay called Nova and said, "Hi Nova, this is Jon from city council. We are doing a quick survey, to know if the neighborhood believes that circumcision can help make stronger men.".

Nova said, "Hey men of my house are already strong and I bet you'd not want to know how strong.".

Jay laughed, "Oh but what about circumcision, I hear it makes real men.".

Nova exhaled, "Is Circumcision some new health plan, because it really sounds cool. But we aren't interested.".

Nova hanged the phone. Seriously this woman thought that their bloodline was pure and that of country's landlords, but she didn't even knew about circumcision. Seriously that was odd. I mean what was this woman from, Mars, or maybe men of her house were from Mars. But one thing was sure that she was in no mood of buying circumcision, so how could she probably give 30 K dollars to an unknown woman to save one of her ancestral enemies. Jay still had doubt on her, and she wasn't going anywhere with this. Now Jay was curious and he wanted know, that if there was some woman who was about to get married to Max but he refused, because this was something that could piss any woman of this world. Seeing Max, one could easily say that he must have got many marriage proposals, so this woman could be one of them. Max knew what Jay was talking about.

There did was such woman and her name was Molly. She was a neighbor of Max and their family had been close ever since they were kid. In fact Charles had always wanted Molly to marry Max. When Max had graduated, Charles had tried everything that Max said yes to marry Molly, but there was Stella in Max's life. All of this had hurt Molly, but she didn't say a word. Molly also was little psychic about Max, or maybe over protective. This was enough for Jay and they drove right outside Molly's house. Max told him about their common friend Bill who has been long gone from the city. Jay called Molly.

Jay said, "Hey Molly, how's it going. It's me Bill. Hey I heard Max is getting married.".

Molly said, "Bill, everyone gets married. Max is no exception, he is just another man.".

Jay said, "Don't tell me that you spent your teenage thinking about just another man.".

Molly said, "Shit happens, so does teenage, and Max is a thing of past.".

Max couldn't believe hearing their conversation. In fact if Stella hadn't came in Max's life, it would have been Molly for sure whom he would have got married to. Seriously, Max felt hurt, listening to Molly that their teenage days were now as good as shit to Molly. If it were to hear Molly, it felt as if she didn't even knew that Max was getting married. Seriously, and she always called herself the best friend of Max. Were best friend supposed to be like this. Like one who can't accept their best friends happiness. For a minute Max thought that he had done wrong to Molly, by keeping her in dark. Right from the start their parents had made them believe that they were just more than a friend. Max very well knew that, and would even flirt with Molly making her believe that someday they will be closer.

But then Stella came in, and maybe this was about moving forward in life. Everybody did that, in fact it sounded like Molly too had moved up in her life. But the question was, who was that wretched woman who was making Max do everything he would never even think of. Max made Jay stop the car in a corner.

Max said, "Hey I don't doubt your skills, but I don't see we getting any closer.".

Jay said, "Max I am a private detective, not Police. So this is how close I can be to a citizen of this city.".

Max whiffed, "What I mean is, they are not just going to shout out loud that hey I am screwing Max.".

Jay said, "Chances are they will never. But trust me, if I go and ask them if they were screwing Max, they would for sure shout out loud. So we have to stay low, and keep an eye. Trust me I am the detective in here.".

Max wasn't getting impatient, but he very well knew that this woman for sure had more questions for Max and more dirty things to do. Hence the sooner they caught her, the better it was for Max. But seriously after having got circumcised, Max do was feeling like a man, in fact a lot more like a man, because for all past few days all his mind could think of was his hanging thing inside his pants. Ah, he had no idea on what she would made him do next, maybe get rid of his hairs just like his favorite actor Brooce Willis. Max had also imagined how would he look like with a bald head, maybe like an old eagle, but definitely not very good looking.

For now Max was unsure that if Jay would be able to find that woman or not, and his mind was saying that maybe he should contact the police, but then Jay was also an ex policemen, that too a fine ex-policeman, so would Police be better than him. Not sure. Now Jay had asked Max, if there was some woman with whom Max had a serious fight with, like a wrangle or dirty exchange of words, who would keep this in her mind. Well, there do was such woman and her name was Ember. Ember was older sister of a girl whom his younger brother Jose had dated for a long time. Jose was young at that time, and made some mistakes with that girl, and then he thought maybe they weren't meant to be together, so he broke up. But Ember made a scene out of it, by visiting Max's house to fight with everybody. She had even slapped Max, to which Max had kicked her as she fell on the stairs out. That day Max had seen fire, yes fire in Ember's eyes. Maybe she was doing this, in spite that it has been pretty long. Both drove to park outside Embers house. Jay called her.

Jay said, "Hi Ember, this is Jon from City council. We have heard from a source that you were recently looking for an organ donor. So we would like to help.".

Ember said, "I have all the organs needed, and two big booties that everybody wants. So I am good.".

Jay said, "Of course you do. But were you looking these organs for someone else.".

Ember said, "Oh I remember. It wasn't organs, but a whole body, precisely some body, I was looking for my sister.".

Jay said, "How lucky your sister is, is she unmarried.".

Ember said, "Oh she is so unmarried and so looking for male organs. I mean men.".

Again this Ember also turned up into a dead end. But something was not so right, I mean she mentioned about her sister, the very girl that had caused that wrangle with Max. So one thing was sure, that she was still World's best elder sister, and having that feat also implied that she could be the same wretched woman in Max's life. Ember might have seemed innocent, but on her house's fence it was written clearly that trespassers will be sued. This was enough as a sign that she was not at all a woman to stay silent. Jay noted something down in his diary and was already thinking of something else to catch up with Ember. While for Max this was getting a little difficult. I mean all these women from past who have been on bitter terms with him, were all coming back at once. This sure was overwhelming, and Max was already feeling guilty. I mean he felt if the woman behind those satellite phones was doing the right thing. Now Jay wanted to know, if some woman from his past had threatened Max. Well there was one such woman and she was Aspen.

Aspen was a founder of startup named Come In, which made a hospitality software for restaurants. Max on behalf of Catalyzers had funded her company, but he later found that education documents of Aspen were forged, so Max reported this all to his seniors and Fraud Control Department of the city. It was then that Aspen had confronted him, and even begged to take back his fraud cases or her life would be ruined. But Max didn't do so, and Aspen lost the ownership of her company, was fined heavily and her career was destroyed. For now she was working as a receptionist in some Head hunting firm in the business district of city. In fact it was the best job she could get with her real educational documents and a fraud case. Both drove to her office, while Jay kept an eye on her, as he called Aspen.

Jay said, "Hi this is Jon from City Search and we are doing a survey for Best Restaurant in the town. Could you please tell us what was the last best meal you had and where.".

Aspen said, "I don't hit restaurants now. It's me n my kitchen, best in town, if you have an award for that.".

Jay said, "Well, but I don't know why Platterina has shared your details for this survey. You must be regular.".

Aspen said, "Yeah I was a regular there, but years back, that too to clear the invoices.".

Aspen said, "By the way tell them I won't mind a complimentary meal delivered to my home.".

This was another dead end, in fact in few words she had told the entire story. This woman was expecting a complimentary meal to be delivered to her home. By the way Platterina was the same restaurant where Max had got beaten up, ah he got into a fight. Max too was sure that if Aspen had that deal of money, I mean 30K dollars to save his father to just have Max circumcised. I mean after losing her company and paying heavy fine, she had become a broke. But again Jay wasn't satisfied, as he had seen the office where she was a receptionist. This head hunting firm had best investors from the city, even better than Catalyzers. This company offered 401K plan, and stock options to employees as stated in the website, so Aspen sure did had more money than she appeared herself to be having. Plus a detective never had to trust on their suspects.

Jay was already thinking on how to take her on a ride, I mean not literally, but get the truth out. As per Jay this woman had all the reasons to destroy Max, in fact she had even threatened him before, and there was nothing at Max's end for her to change her mind. These were all women that had high index of suspicion. For others Jay sat in his office to call them at his comfort, while all Max did was watching him do it. Today Max's past was all flashing in his eyes. All those women, of some loved by Max, some hated by Max, some fantasized by Max eh, some a nightmare for Max, and like that. Jay kept calling.

Jay said, "Hi this is Jon from City Bank, are you interested in an offshore account. Of course to keep your money at bay from Govt. sharks.".

Jay said, "Hi this is Jon from Cross Line Hospital. Yesterday you enquired about a patient. We've an update.".

Jay said, "Hi this is Jon from Nightindale PD. We have hoodlums who have confessed that you hired them.".

Jay said, "Hi this is Jon from city council, you have a pending parking ticket from Cross Line Hospital.".

Jay said, "Hi this is Jon from Platterina. Your last time visit has won you a complementary dinner for two.".

This went on and Jay kept making notes of all highs and lows of the suspects, to shorten this list of 70 women. But every other woman was now looking suspicious. What piqued Jay the most was that each of these women were different than the other, which meant that Max did had a taste for diversity. I mean you could only make relationships with people that are similar to you, or make contact with people that are similar to you. But Max looked like a man who didn't saw any differences, which had raised Jay's brow. Both were sure that this woman would be calling Max soon and this time they had to be prepared.

The day was soon over, and it was almost night, and now Max was back in his home. Seriously it was no longer a home without Stella. She was gone, the marriage was called off, and there was no body in the home to snuggle into. Even his dog was feeling little depressed. This wretched woman had taken away what Max loved the most, and Max was not stopping till he had Stella back in his life. The bedroom was empty, so was the wardrobe, so was the kitchen, and the dishes in sink had gone. A strange emptiness had crept in and again this night had become sleepless.

Chapter 7

After few days of gap, karma was calling, wait karma wasn't the best word to be used especially if some woman from past was on your back. It was work. Max was again back to his office, to be surrounded by same nerdy startup founders. Problems, ideas and solutions it was. But Max's head was somewhere else. Could it be Nina, but she was a police officer, I mean since when did Policemen ah policewomen started making citizens do crime. But then Nina would have all the required contacts to pull this off. Max even questioned the fact that did Nina ever loved him or had a real crush on him or was it just obsession. But seriously a girl like Nina who hesitated to propose Max for all those years was now a policewomen, that was a shocker. I mean she had done exceptionally well with her life. But Hadn't Max did well in his life too. Maybe Nina couldn't just accept the fact that Max was doing well even without her. God this was a shame moment of manhood that Max was thinking about women from his past just to know who had been screwing his present.

It was not just these women that have been bothering Max. It was also the atmosphere, while everybody was looking at Max as a hero who had just fired Oscar, it was only Max who knew what he was feeling from inside. In fact today Max was missing Oscar, his high pitch voice, his slamming the door whenever he left Max's office, wait that was so rude and Oscar deserved to be fired. In mid of this his phone rang. Holy hell, this was not happening that soon. It was another satellite phone number.

Woman said, "Max, it is time for some real man fun. But tell me first, what is most fun for men.".

Max said, "Seriously, taking my father to the verge of death is so not fun.".

Woman clichéd, "Max that was the source of manhood, what makes a man a man, remember.".

Max said, "Of course. And I bet that cracking some good old jokes is not fun for you, ah real men.".

Woman said, “Break a bone. Yes, you go, break a bone or say a leg and be a man. But the leg has to be of a Harley driver. You know the rugged macho people. Remember that night I got you beaten up in restaurant. Of course you do. Now this is your chance to settle the score. You know how. Those men too were Harley driver, and I am not telling you this so you could tell this to your private detective. Though the fun part in here is that if you don’t do so, Jack or maybe Jeff will have to lose their legs in lieu. So all the best, ah, just, break a bone or break a leg.”.

The woman hanged, and all Max could do was not believe on his fate. He wanted to hit the mobile phone on his head, but it was of no use, as he had to break a bone not a mobile phone. Seriously, this woman was mad. Now what should Max do, save Jack, or save Jeff, or just catch up a Harley driver and break his legs. Seriously and the Harley driver would say, hey man I was born to be broken a leg by you, do it, it is all yours. This was really getting intense. I mean getting circumcised was easier, and so was firing Oscar, but now he had to really break a bone that too leg.

I mean if breaking a leg made you a man, then there would be hardly thousand men in this city, and what were rest, some self doubting humans. God, no way Max was going to do this. This woman should know that Max was not her puppet. He took his phone and kept it on silent. God, when will this end, when will Max have no such obsessive woman in his life. But wait, Jay should definitely know what this woman was up to. Before Max could pick his phone, his phone rang, and thankfully it was Jack.

Jack said, “Max swear by my friendship, that you won’t fund any alcoholic startups.”.

Max said, “Seriously, I am at work Jack. Don’t break your retarded jokes now.”.

Jack said, “Bro, I was this close to be retarded forever. A drunkard hit me straight in my legs, by his car. A freaking car. I mean how could he not see me, and how could you not see through my piteous voice. You both are same. Wait, I hope you aren’t drunk now.”.

Max held his head, "Hey, please tell me, this was a joke. Because that woman had called, and warned me so.".

Meanwhile Max's cell phone rang and the woman said, "You don't have much time Max.".

Now I don't even have time, great. Max took his jacket and was already out to see Jack. He had also called Jay to the hospital Jack was in. God, where was this going. This woman had already started getting so physical. I mean circumcision, and now break a leg. Someone had to stop this woman. Max slammed his hands on his steering thinking what the hell Jay was doing. Weren't private detectives paid a lot to find the culprits faster than police. I mean she actually did it, just to prove her point. She made Jack look like a goat, or precisely a guinea pig. If Max would not do this, who would stop her from taking away Jack's both legs. This woman was dragging his friends, his family and everyone close, because she knew that Max would do anything for them. She was always right on spot. Max had reached the hospital, and there was Jack lying in bed craped in bandages, while Jay was trying to calm down Jack and bring some sense back to him.

Jay said, "So now this woman wants you to break a leg, or our mutual friend Jack will lose his legs mutually."

Jack said, "Oh don't tell me, that another drunkard will soon hit me again at my legs. God that will hurt.".

Max snapped back, "And you idiot couldn't even see his license plate. I wonder who was blind.".

Jack screeched, "Max, I was drunk. I mean he was drunk. Didn't spotting this was enough. And wait, me in this hospital with bruised legs is only because 3 years back I had a drink with person named Max, and it is the hangover of that friendship which has broken now, as I see your real face. You are not a friend.".

Max said, "Jay, you know I can't do this. I can't break a bone of someone I don't know, I don't even hate.".

Jack interrupted, "Here he said it, hate. You know Jay, he did enjoyed firing Oscar. That woman was right he enjoyed fulfilling his hatred. He is that kind of man, but not my friend.".

Max said, "Can't we go to the police, before I actually commit a crime.".

Jay said, "Being an ex-policemen, I can bet, you won't get better expertise than mine, choice is yours.".

Were there some moments when everything felt unreal. Yes there were, and this moment was the same as for Max. Break a leg, Max had never even dreamt that he would do it literally. Settling the score, seriously, this woman sure didn't had better excuse to justify this act. Max who was still in disbelief, was now eyeing outside the window, and then at piteous face of Jack. Max didn't had drinks with him 3 years back, to leave him alone with broken legs. So there it was, Max decided that he would do it. He would do it for Jack, he would do it to save Jack's legs. He would do it for friendship, he would do it for becoming a man, wait, becoming a man so that woman finally leaves Max out of this.

Max and Jay were now headed to the Highway 59. This was Jay's idea, as this place was full of Harley drivers driving in and out of city. Catching one of them wasn't difficult. Max had parked his car just outside a diner with lots of Harley's parked outside. Seriously, was this fun, Max doubted himself. No this was no fun, especially if he missed breaking the legs, he would get broken up badly by those Harley drivers. Max was catching up with his breaths, I mean he had never done anything like that before. But he was thankful that Jay had accompanied him. All his life Max used to feel disgust with people breaking baseball bats with ones, but now he was soon going to become one of them. Max cleared his head and turned back to Jay.

Max said, "Now what am I supposed to do. I mean give me some hints, not like that woman.".

Jay said, "Take it easy. Just wait for some stud to drive out his Harley. Follow him to a distance where there is no one around, and SLAM your car towards his leg. And this is all about breaking the leg bone. The woman will be pleased, Jack will be safe, and I am not sure if you will have some fun in it or not.".

Max said, "I thought you were a detective I hired to make this woman stop.".

Jay snapped back, “No stopping, I see a driver coming out. I’m stepping out. But keep a focus on those legs.”.

Max said, “Seriously his legs. Most probably they wouldn’t be even shaved.”.

Jay stepped out to stand in corner of that diner, as it was Max who was to become man and of course hitting that man with Jay alongside would have pissed the woman. The rider on the other end of parking was drunk and swaying like winter winds. Seriously, was Max about to hit a man when he was drunk, this was so death of manhood, but if he wouldn’t hit the man that still be death of manhood as per woman and as for not able to save his friend Jack. The rider lighted a cigarette and went on to drive in opposite direction, out of the city. Max followed him and kept a close distance with the rider. God, was he seriously about to hit another man whom he didn’t even knew, was this some game, yes game for sure, but there wasn’t any fun in it as he saw. Max waited till the driver was way off the reach of diner. Meanwhile the Harley driver had stopped Max and curiously abused him ‘You Fucker.’. That was it, the man inside Max had risen and maybe there do was some fun in getting this wreck on bed.

Max paced his car and bumped into his leg rest area. The Harley went dragging down the highway, while Max took a U turn to race back to Jay and pick him off the route. People said that there always are some moments that define your life, and this was one of it. Max turned the radio on and it was his favorite song playing, Highway Hell. God damn, it felt good to be relieved of that woman’s threats. Seriously it felt like a video game. Max was so worried on how he would do it, but guess what it was even simpler than getting circumcised. Max wasn’t sure if this woman was going up the level, or the game was about to end by going down. Max and Jay headed back to hospital to Jack’s bed.

Max said, “Hey, I just broke a leg so you could keep kicking beer cans. And yes you are welcome.”.

Jack said, “I knew you would do it, as you are the man. I mean brother, and a brother has to be a man.”.

Jay said, “Hey, hey, hey. We all are men, but don’t forget the woman behind us.”.

Max said, “He is right. She needs to be taken care of, and Jay you seriously got to change places with this woman. I mean you are here to be behind her, not the other way.”.

Jack said, “Ah, that will bring her in between. Like a burger, will she be comfortable.”.

Max hit on his bandaged legs while Jack laughed, and then rang Max’s phone. Max held his head thinking god this can’t be happening. It was the woman calling from another satellite number. The happiness of these three men was indeed short lived, and this woman was still behind these men, running the cards. Max picked it.

Woman said, “I am disappointed Max. This is the second time you didn’t do it right. The first was circumcision in bathroom, and now this. The man you hit, is now hitting the road to Vegas. His legs didn’t broke, apart from some swelling in muscles. And that was not what I meant, and this is definitely not funny. I assume that you aware about how serious business we are in.”.

Max said, “Now who do you think I am, a doctor with a portable X Ray machine.”.

Woman said, “Max, to stay in a brotherhood, you have to ruin a brother. This is how it works. Now you are going to break a leg for real, like hitting on some Harley Drivers leg with a baseball bat, till you hear a crack. Now this is how it is going to be. Your time has already started.”. She hung up.

Max kept yelling back, “Hear a crack, seriously, should I do it in a studio and record the sounds.”.

Jay said, “Don’t tell me, we are doing this again. Have you ever played baseball, just asking.”.

Max said, “Not we Jay, but me. You are just going to take another corner. By the way this stupid hit and run idea of yours has clearly failed. And Jack, your legs got to be priceless, because you have no idea on how I am paying for them. I know a place where to find Harley Drivers, lots of them.”.

To err is human, which means to err is also manly. But this woman surely didn’t agreed with the statement. So here it was, breaking another leg till Max heard a crack. The place that

Max was talking about was Whimshire, a nearby hilly village where Max often drove to freshen himself up. At the starting of this village there was a bar, which was a popular hangout point of many highway riders, and every time Max drove there he always saw dozens of Harley parked outside. Max knew that this was the place because often in that bar people fought, tore their clothes and broke the furniture. On a whole it was shady bar, and what this woman wanted now could only be done in this place.

Seriously, what was Max becoming a serial leg breaker, and all this because of Jack who would never be as thankful to Max as Max took it to him. But this was how men saved and nurtured their friendship, maybe this was how it was meant to be. They were driving to Whimshire while Max couldn't help but look at Jay. Seriously this man was a detective, and instead of catching that woman he was now sitting with Max trying to help so eventually that woman could make her point, wasn't this pointless. Max remembered Stella, and how mad she would be at Max if she got to know all about this. God, he was not so telling her. They have the reached the Hill Side Bar, well that was its name, Hill Side. Max parked the car and took a deep breath.

Max said, "How can I thrash a man's leg, one even I don't know of. This is insane.".

Max shrugged, "You know Jay, I am not that kind of man. I don't know if that kind even exists.".

Jay snapped back, "Look, I have an idea. Trust me on this one. I know you are not paying me to give you ideas on how to make the woman win. But the choice was yours, and if you hear me out, you will find some sense to keep away the guilt. And this idea is for free.".

Max didn't have a leather jacket, but hell he looked like a man, as he entered the bar by slamming the doors to make heads turn around. Max still had blood dropping down his cheeks, of course not the real blood, but one that only the man himself could feel after hitting another man so hard that he least had some muscle injuries. Max looked around giving a tough guy vibes, while he couldn't believe he was actually doing this. But his head was clear and he knew exactly what he had to do. He passed by a table where few men were playing poker, and Max placed a hundred dollar on a man's side he saw the cards of. He said no words and kept moving on towards the bar table.

He gestured for two shots of vodka with lime. Max couldn't have afforded to look weak, or his plan would have blown. He took out his wallet which was jam packed with money to pay for the drinks while he sat with few rugged men close by him. Particularly next to a young twenty something man. Both eyed each other and Max ordered another round of shots for him. This was no showing off, but had a little bit of showing involved as Max had already seen a huge chain around his pockets with a leather strap of Harley. So this was the man, he was a Harley driver, a right pick, who had himself walked up to Max. I mean what could have been better than this.

The young Harley man said, "You are not from around, so what brings you here.".

Max said, "Of course I don't live around, so that has brought me here. The hill and the men.".

The Harley rider said, "Ha that was wicked. Hills I understand, but we are not that kind of men.".

Max shook his head in dismay, "Oh, men don't have a kind. Trust me. They all are as same as one. By the way, there is one more thing that got me here. I need to break a leg bone.".

Harley rider stiffened, "Oh that won't be easy, though Hill Side people serve dinner within 10. Try that.".

Max snapped back, "This is why I am going to need you.".

With this Max took a bundle of 100 dollar bills and placed it right next to the drink of that Harley rider. The Harley rider first looked at the bundle, which was overwhelming considering the side of this town, and then he looked back at Max. This was a good deal, and the Harley rider couldn't just refuse free money. He grabbed the bundle and kept it in his pocket. He finished his drink and shook hands with Max. Seriously, was it going to be that easy, Max had never thought. Jay really was some wicked piece with all these ideas. Both were now headed back to their rides. Max got on his car, while the young man started his

Harley, while Jay was hiding in a phone booth near the bar. This Whimshire that had always appeared to be a shady place to Max had turned out pretty co-operative.

Chapter 8

Whimshire was a small city, but still Max had been driving for last 15 minutes. They were now at the footsteps of hills, the real hills. Max was not still sure whether he'd be able to do it or not. What if this young rider took Max out, seriously that would be epic, because back at the bar it was Jay who would spend another 2 days in finding him. Thoughts of mere slashing that baseball bat were giving him chills. Seriously did men break a leg to have fun. I mean if it was some play station game it would have made sense for once. Max looked out of the window, and waved hands to the rider who was riding carelessly with a cigarette stubbed between his lips. Max couldn't believe he was about to send this man to hospital for another couple of days, and this was no public service nor did this man had any contagious disease. Max stopped at a pre fixed ground that had jungle beyond it, and so did the rider stopped his bike. Okay, so now the time had come to have some fun. Max picked up the baseball bat from behind, and stepped out. It was dark, and only the headlights were lit.

The rider said, "Hey where is that man, you want break a leg of. I don't see anybody. Is he on way.".

Max came closer, "Seriously, why did you think I got you here all this WAY. Now gimme your legs.".

With that Max hit hardest he could the bat on rider's leg. The rider crippled down on just the first blow. He screamed with pain, but it was only the jungles to overhear him.

The rider said, "You crazy coward, don't you dare hit me again. I've friends back in bar and they won't need any money to break yours. Trust me, you too are bounded by karma.".

Max kept beating him and then heard a crack, "Hey I just heard a crack. Did your leg got broken.".

The Harley rider said, "You dumb head, it is not my leg but your bat that has cracked.".

Max kept him beating, till he heard another crack, and now he was sure that his leg were broken. With every blow Max was becoming into some person whom Max would have hated. Was this fun, yes eventually Max realized that it do was some fun, in beating the shit out of a rowdy man. Max didn't only cracked his leg, but thrashed his Harley too, by yelling back at him, 'Now try going back to that bar with a broken leg'. The breaking of Harley was complimentary. I mean Max hadn't thought about it. But he hated the fact why such bikes were even made, if it weren't these bikes, such men like this rider won't be there, and that woman wouldn't have given Max such an act to do. In fact, if Harley's factory was nearby, Max would have put it on fire. Plus Max didn't wanted to be chased to his home.

Finally Jack's legs were now safe, and Max had did well as a friend, a man friend. Breaking a leg was something he wouldn't be proud of, but saving a friend sure did was. Max waited in his car, while Jay and Jack were having beer in river front. Max was thinking maybe this woman would call again, probably to bid a goodbye, or probably to say that Max had done well. Wait, was now Max thinking about this woman. He sure did was, wait this was no sign of affection, Stella still was the only woman of his life. Stella too had made Max feel like a man on those lonely nights. This woman could never replace Stella, but something about her was so mystical. God, Max went back to his home, to only sip another 2 bottles of wine and sleep like few things were taken care of. Day passed by, and it was Jay knocking back on his door with Jack alongside. They got together in the living room.

Jay said, "I have my first findings about this case. Nina doesn't works in Police. She lied.".

Jay continued, "Your girl Anna, who was pretending to be too cute for anything, has a new hot boyfriend that has an account in bank of Isles. So he doesn't finds her accountable, NO. She lied.".

Jay said, "Now lets get to Nova, or Mrs. Smith, or godmother of your grandfather. She lied too, as it has been only a year that she had got her son circumcised. I wonder next time she doesn't says, hey what is cock, it sounds pretty cool, is it a name for non-vegan bananas.".

Jay continued, "Now this is interesting. I hacked into Molly's Facebook account and saw a conversation between her and Daisy. Molly knew that marriage was called off, but she didn't say a word then. She is red flag, as she regularly talks to Daisy, and guess what most of it is about you.".

Jay said, "Ember's sister was already engaged. And I guess now she is finding a sheikh for her.".

Jay continued, "Aspen visited Platterina just a week before. In fact she had shared a picture of her on social media with some fusion dish and sparkling teeth covered by some dental plan.".

Jay exhaled, "Max its sad to say, but all women in your life from past are twisted bitches. They all lied.".

Jack said, "Seriously, and one of these woman wants Max to be a Man. That's a serial lie.". He laughed.

Max said, "Not funny Jack. Hey, so what do we do? They lied about it, so I assume they are hiding something. But of all, our woman is one of them and she knows that I have hired you, a detective. She would be expecting us, in fact all that you found might be another lie. How do we get to her?".

Jay raised his brows, as the answer to Max's question was in his question. Getting to her was only possible by getting to all of these woman. Now Jay and Max had to tail all these women until that woman was exposed. This was the only way of stopping her and new found miseries of Max's life. Now Max had started imagining what would that woman look like from one of the women from his past. Nina was such a quiet, composite girl, i mean what could possibly turn her into such a monster. Seriously, this was how rejected girls avenged their crushes. Seriously and for all these two three days Max thought that Nina had become a respectable person in society by being a policeman, ah Police woman. But why would she lie about being in Police. I mean sooner or later her lie would get exposed.

Ah, life can be so unpredictable, as Max and Jay were again outside Nina's house, the same house that Max had always preferred to avoid whenever he passed by as a kid, just not to give wrong signals. But there it was, she avenging him. Wait, they both spotted Nina talking to a bulky man right on door. They exchanged kisses. This was dubious, as Nina was never so comfortable around men, in fact even around Max her crush. The man handed her a bag full of what they couldn't see through and walked out. Jay clicked his pictures and both stepped out to confront him.

Jay said, "Hey man. Just wanted to ask you, apart from visiting this neighborhood, visiting this house, seeing beautiful Nina, what else you do, because I saw you giving her some shit.".

The bulky man said, "Its Victor, and I am policeman, and trust me its better you stay from that shit.".

Jay laughed, "Is that really you, or her company, because she too thinks she is in Police. Ha.".

Victor pulled his badge from his pockets, "I am from the Public surveillance department. Trust me, Nina is a starter. I have got way better company you would not want to see.".

Jay winked back and patted on Victor's back, to turn around walk into the car and drive away. Jay slammed on the steering and shrugged to Max. Both knew that this was it. I mean Nina was a friend to a man who had access to all public CCTV cameras of the city. No wonder on how Max was being watched all the time. But something else piqued Max, how did she managed to watch him while he was in Catalyzers. Who knows, she might be sitting in the lobby. Keeping an eye on Nina had worked. In fact Jay had revealed that he had seen Victor a day earlier driving around the nearby streets. So one thing was sure that Victor and Nina were in regular touch, and a somber girl like Nina would not have super bowl, or Tarantino movie to talk about with him, so it was obvious she was having some other more interesting conversation.

But Max couldn't believe that actually a policeman was helping Nina, well but then there was lot to be found about, as this was just the starting. Nina had raised a red flag, and she couldn't be ignored now on, as opposite to her teenage days. Though Max was sure that it was Nina behind the curtains, but Jay insisted that they kept an eye on others too, as this could have been a hoax.

The next woman on radar was Anna, the ex-girlfriend. Ah, the exes were the most trickiest one, as they would always overwhelm you with memories of past. So Jay suggested that Max shouldn't see her again and rather they should visit the accountant of Anna, who could tell them about those 30K dollars. I mean this was the best a detective would want to hear. Jay had already found out that this man handled the finances of both Anna and her boyfriend. In fact it was her boyfriend that had introduced him to Anna. Anna was always sweet to Max, but the question was whether she could have stung him too. Jay and Max visited their accountant who was busy in his computers. By the way his name was Leroy.

Jay said, "You know Leroy, it was always makes me sad that accountants multiplies numbers of their clients all their life, but all they get is a percentage.".

Leroy looked up, "And you must be a noble laureate in mathematics.".

Jay laughed, "Yeah, you can say so. We are sort of noble clients, obviously not interested in making money, but are just curious about few numbers of your clients Anna. By the way this man will take care of your numbers, if only you help us with her numbers. Well not the numbers of her dresses to be clear.".

Leroy smiled and pulled a file out, "Okay i can tell you about her transactions. Last week she has liquefied 50k dollars for some personal finance, but hasn't bought or invested in anything. Then 25 days back she made an investment in Equity funds. And her EMI's for new car is always on time, and.".

Jay interrupted, "Hey that will be it. Here is your 3K dollars. You know, being not a noble always pays.".

They walked out, Jay said. "50K dollars disappear, while her boyfriend has an account in Bank of Isles.".

Max said, "One doesn't has to have noble prize in mathematics to figure that.".

Seriously what could be the reason so immediate that Anna needed 50K Dollars. She already had a car, and still she hadn't moved into a new apartment, she had no debtors chasing her back or her accountant must have known. This was another level of suspicion. But why were Nina and Anna both looking suspicious. Maybe one of them had bad co incidence behind her, and the other was culprit. But keeping an eye on all these women was so needed at this hour. Max still remembered on how calculative Anna was with her finances, in fact she never wasted a single penny on anything until it was necessary, and now she had 50K dollars vanished up in air. She was a duly honest tax paying citizen, and would never launder the money, unless she wanted to screw Max for leaving her. When they had broken up, Anna had gone in depression and didn't left her apartment for straight 1 month as friends had told. God, even Anna was cute and good looking, then why did Max had to leave her to create trouble for himself in future. Wait, was this heading to getting together again with Anna. Damn, Exes always overwhelmed you, it was so right.

Jay was now headed to Molly's house. As per Jay's sources, it appeared that Molly was under some sort of House arrest as she would not step out of her house for days in straight. Seriously this might sound odd, but for Jay it was enough that she had a headquarter bunker in her basement to carry out all nasty things. Jay somehow had to find, what was Molly up to. They both parked the car outside her house, and it has been almost half an hour but there was no sign of her. Jay stepped out of the car and so did Max.

Jay laughed, "Max you are so unlucky to have refused marrying her and be voided of an In house wife.".

Max said, "Ah, we were this close then, now here I am working with an agency to get to her nerves.".

Jay said, "I mean seriously, how did even your parents got their eyes on this Cinderella. Wait.".

A mail man dropped by and placed an envelop in her mail box, seeing this Jay hurried along with Max to check the mail box. It could have led them somewhere. It was full of letters and Jay opened all of them one by one. There it was, and Jay smiled patting the letter on Max's chest.

Jay said, "Response to a query from Organ Donor bank. Guess who else was finding a liver.".

Max held his head, "God, my parents gave her their hearts. Wasn't that enough.".

Nina, Anna and Now Molly, no one was clean. They had hands smudged in dirt, and now they have got Jay and Max both to think, on actually who was that woman. They all had activities suspicious of being that woman. But seriously, Molly should have remained in her house and not sought such adventures for Max. Well anyway it was good for her, as she wouldn't find uncomfortable in jail, having spent all time indoor, because this was not ending here. These all three women were up on Jay's radar. In this case all of the suspects were looking as dubious as one suspect could get. All of them were up to something, but there was only one that was hiding amidst all this. The letter had clearly said, that we are sorry, but we do not have any active liver donor for now. Max reconsidered his thoughts that twisted bitches was indeed an understatement for these women, or precisely one of them.

Now the question was who was it. But before that Jay wanted to check up with the other suspects too. So next up the list was Ember, the older sister, the protective sister, and a woman who can arouse interest in any man. Seriously Jay hadn't wondered, if only Ember and Max would have met in some normal circumstances, chances were Ember would have totally got him. They both waited outside Ember's house, and finally a rugged man walked out. Jay went up to him.

Jay said, "Hey, hope you don't mind me asking, as anyways you don't look like man driven by mind. Ha just kidding, but what is between you and Ember.".

The rugged man said, "She is my woman. So stay away, unless you won't mind your mind.".

Another man following him stopped, "Seriously, are you from some chicken farm, you don't know Diddy.".

Jay smiled, "If I'd be from chicken from, I'd sure have known diddy.".

Diddy's escort said, "He owns these streets, by all means, he is also their contractor.".

Jay called his old friend from the same neighborhood, who told him that Diddy was the local don. It raised an alarm to both Max and Jay. If he was a don, then Max getting beaten up that night made some sense. I mean with Diddy by her side, Ember could have easily pulled all off this. So this woman Ember was not only an elder sister but the first woman of this neighborhood too. I mean how twisted a woman could be than this. Seriously, Max was going to get back home and lecture Jose on picking the right people in his life. Clearly a woman who can date the shadiest person of the neighborhood could do anything, and dating her younger sister would be an unsaid crime for a straight man. Straight as in, sorted man. They weren't sure, but maybe this was the source of all those baseball men that had beaten up Max that night.

This was surely getting somewhere, though Jay insisted that they kept looking all the women. So now next up the list was Nova. The mature woman, who would sure not be dating another underworld man. They reached their house, while Jay couldn't help but see the lines of houses besides her up till Max's parental house that actually once belonged to Nova's family. Seriously, all this loss, even Jay would be so pissed to make Max's life hell. This was an unreasonable reason. They waited, and saw with binoculars to the living room where Nova was busy making calls. After a while she left the house and drove her car to the city center, then to the business district, while Jay and Max followed her. She had stopped and now was walking on foot, with Max and Jay at a safe distance right behind her.

Max said, "Hey I am not feeling right, this is too close. Plus she can call the police for stalking.".

Jay snapped back, "Oh come on, Police wouldn't believe that. I mean stalkers too have a standard.".

Max said, "You think it's funny, My father was about to lose his life.".

Jay said, "Think about her father, he lost 7 houses. You think that is funny. You know Max, in city we live in, a house is way costlier than a man's life. This woman has got all the reasons, and I am not leaving her trail.".

Within few minutes, she had now entered a huge tall building. They both followed, until she rode a lift inside. Max stopped Jay, while he looked up to the top floor. Max was in total dismay, and stopped Jay from following further.

Max held his head and said, “Jay, this office building belongs to Alpha AI.”

Chapter 9

It has to be an inside man. I mean how could that woman know that Alpha AI had outstanding debts, unless that woman had her neck inside them, and there it was Nova being spotted inside Alpha AI. Damn, why didn't Max thought that this leak could have been from Alpha AI, and all these days he worried if that Woman had some person working for her inside Catalyzers. Max had always been the face of his family, and this woman was now taking down to him. God, this so made sense as the founder of Alpha AI was also an immigrant and had spent his childhood in the same neighborhood, maybe he was helping Nova. But for sure Max was not going to ask him that. Nova, Nova, Nova, she still couldn't get over the fact that it was Government not those poor immigrant families that took her houses.

Of all this, today Jay had proved his worth as he had winning smile on his face with that many leads. But wait, it wasn't over, as they still had to eye Aspen. The last of most suspected women. As per Jay's sources, Aspen had gone to see the doctor, and Jay had planned to visit her office and maybe find something about her. They had driven as fast as they could, because Nova had already drilled delay in their schedule. This time Jay and Max both entered her office, passing by her chair which was today occupied by the office guard. Jay spotted a man in his late twenties who was checking out one of her colleagues. He looked like a womanizer, so chances were he had known a lot about Aspen too. They approached him.

Jay said, "Hey, she is really sexy. You got some great eyes. You should be scouting models.".

The colleague said, "No, no, no, if you don't find her sexy then you got to be blind, and you should be staying in some social care hospital for differently abled.".

Jay said, "Let's pretend we're at right place. Have you noticed anything unusual about Aspen.".

The colleague said, "You know I've also got a great voice, and I am calling the guard.".

Max grabbed his collar, "Last night I've broken a leg, and I'm sure you don't want to get in between.".

The colleague calmed his hands trying to sober him down, while Max left his collar. Wait, was that Oscar. Max ducked into the cubicle, while trying to catch a better glimpse of, oh yes, that was Oscar. Wait, Oscar got a job here. Max took Jay by his hands, and they both strode out.

Max said, "That was Oscar, the man I fired because of that woman.".

Jay snapped back, "Relax Max, he is not that man that woman is after. Getting it.".

I mean what in the world was that. Aspen worked in a highly reputable firm, and these people don't even let employees join the office without proper document, while Oscar got a job here after Max had written the worst of relieving letters. Was this all a ploy, just to make Max feel like the bad man. What the hell was this woman up to, or what was Aspen if she was that woman, up to. She gave Oscar a job after he was fired by him. If this was it, then what was the point of making him fire Oscar. I mean with all this Max was not getting closer to become a better man for sure.

Insane, insane, insane, maybe this woman was just sick, or maybe sick of Max. I mean what did Max had done in his life to piss of any woman he had known. Max was doing his job when he revoked Aspen's company's funding. There was nothing personal about it, in fact it was ethically good business for Catalyzers. Jay left Max at his home, while again tonight Max drank another two bottles of wine. Maybe this poison would help beat the poison that woman was feeding her with. The night went on, and Max was sitting on his couch with shimmering eyes to the sunlight coming in from windows. The television was on. Wait was that same rider. Oh shoot. The rider Max had broken leg of was all over the TV.

The news anchor said, "So who is this Harley Hunter. A poor Harley Driver looses his legs for another couple of months, after getting thrashed by an unknown man. What is this madness our country is driving into. Wait, only few hours back, another

Harley driver was also hit by some unknown man. We suspect that they both are connected.".

A spokesperson Of Harley was also on TV, "I think its our competitors, trying to scare people into buying our bikes. But you know what men aren't made in factories, they are born. Now try stopping men from being born."

Another Harley rider said on TV, "This is a man thing, not driving Harley, of course it is, but breaking a man's leg. I think this assaulter thinks he is a man above the crest. But guess what he can break our legs, but not our spirits. We will still rule the highways, and will make pit stops to every bar en route.".

A policeman said, "This man is a psychic criminal. Maybe his father was an abusive alcoholic Harley driver, who never took him on a ride. But we will. This man is not going anywhere.".

Max shut off the TV, and held his head. These last few days have been crazier than super bowl finals, wait no super bowl, as Max was never again going to buy another baseball bat. God now the police was also on his tail, and what if they caught him. I mean what would Max say, that he was trying to become a man because one woman from his past wanted him to. Seriously, these acts now had to stop. Max no more cared if that woman would break Jack's both legs. I mean as a good friend, Max would gift him a wheelchair even if there weren't Christmas around. This just had to stop. In all of his life he had never imagined, that some woman, some woman from his past would be running the strings of his life. Seriously, this had to stop. Max was already missing Stella, Daisy, Esther, Dad, and Mom. He had avoided all their calls for last few days. Without his family he was feeling breathless. Max's phone rang. Hell no.

The woman said, "Max, what it is that drives a man go crazy?".

Max said, "I assume I have become a man now, and you are driving me crazy. This ends here.".

The woman said, "It's a good fuck Max, not what I am doing to you, but the answer.".

Max snapped back, "You know, I've had many good fucks in my life, and will have more with Stella. Cool.".

The woman said, "You are not getting my point Max. What you have with Stella is making love, with passion, desire, and more compassion. What I want you to do is, Fuck, simply fuck, no emotions involved. So now you are going to fuck an unknown woman, and she can't be a slut, or you can't pay her, nor can you propose her. You are doing this or else I am uploading a sex tape of your sister on internet. Have a look.".

Max snapped back, "What did you do with my sister. Just leave her out.".

The woman said, "Oh, this tape is of her with her boyfriend. I didn't do anything with her, nor my rugged men, though they would love to, But no. And yes, we will leave her out of the internet, if you do as I say.".

Max threw his phone towards the wall, and sat on his couch holding his head. God this was crazy, and this was not done. This wretched woman was now dragging his family into this become a man crap, first his father, now his sister. I mean she had to be stopped, or she would ruin everything that Max and his family had built for years. This was no normal, and some great hard hitting grudge. Wait, that woman had to be stopped. Max rushed to pick his phone and put back the scattered pieces. He turned his phone on, and thankfully it was working. He opened his messenger and there it was the short clip, with a short message, 'Censored for a beloved brother'.

Seriously this woman was doing nothing but digging her own grave, till she found she was so going in it. Max played the file. By the way it was her younger sister, Claudia, not Daisy. Claudia was studying in Williamson University. She was the youngest of all siblings and most loved too. Max played the video. Body of Claudia was blurred, while she was talking off her clothes with some young dude who was totally naked while Max could even see few hairs on his back. He forwarded the video and there it was, these both making out, while Claudia was yelling, Yes Phillip, Come faster, Yes Phillip. Again, Max felt like throwing the phone on wall, thinking they were committing some sin. But it wasn't. Seriously, someone was making this video while all this went. Oh god, how stupid Claudia was, or maybe her brother Max was stupid. But seriously, how did this woman got hands on this video. Max made a call to her.

Max said, "Hey who is this Philip, and how can you have sex with him.".

Claudia snapped back, "Brother calm down. He is my boyfriend, and having sex with boyfriends is normal. What do you want me to do, maybe sleep with some random person from street.".

Max said, "No, you are not supposed to sleep with anyone. We sent you to the college for studying Marketing, and not making out. Anyways, don't tell anyone back in home that we had this conversation.".

There it was, sleep with some random person from street. Max had no option but to do that. This was the most embarrassing moment a brother could get in. Seriously how could Claudia do this to Max. Her sex tape going viral was the last thing he would want to happen in the world, even after his death. God, now how was Max supposed to fuck a woman, I mean this was like raping somebody with only difference that you had consent for it, and there was no violence involved. God, I mean which woman in the world would let Max fuck her like if it was as normal as buying a coffee, wait he couldn't even buy that. For sure this woman was testing Max's mettle, and he was not backing out especially if his sister was at stake.

God, Max felt like calling a friend, but his hands hesitated, I mean how would he explain this to Jack or Jeff that there was some sex tape made of his sister. Seriously, they would not say it on his face, but will know that Claudia was a slut. Shit, Max couldn't have asked for help from anyone. Seriously what was this Jay doing, apart from keeping an eye. Max couldn't even tell this to Daisy, or Fred would create a scene and screw all this up. This sex tape and this secret had to die with Max, and that woman. There was nothing else to it. But seriously, Claudia was so going to have it this time from Max. He literally felt like bring her back to home, and get her married to some nice man. Max's phone rang, hell no, it was Jack.

Jack said, "Hey Max, last night I dreamt about. Not like if we were making out in that dream. But you just came in, and said, Hey Jack help me, I am so screwed. And I said, Max I didn't do anything. Seriously, this was the strangest dream I ever had. For first time I dreamt about a man. Something special must be about to happen.".

Max said, "Oh so all you do is dream about women. This is where all your action happens.".

Jack said, "Hey man, I dreamt about you. Isn't it cool as a friend, and you are roasting me.".

Max chuckled, "Yeah its cool, I mean lot real too. As anyways you don't get to do anything.".

Jack said, "Ha, ha, ha. Guess what, with woman like that in your life, I would love doing nothing. Okay, wait, that was my bad. Didn't wanted to hurt you.".

Max said, "Its fine Jack. Hey listen, I wanted to tell you something. I am leaving the city for a day or two. Something very important has come up. Okay. But tell Jay to keep things rolling as he is still active on my payroll. Once I will be back we will meet and try figure out doing something solid about your dream, of course the woman.".

Max hung up the phone, shit he just couldn't tell his best friend that this woman was up with some new drama. Does fucking a woman really drives men crazy. Seriously, thanks to this enlightening woman, Max had now known some new and novel man theories. I mean Max never went crazy to fuck someone. This was something that felt good when came in easy and naturally. Max cleared his head and opened his smart phone to search in Google, 'Where to find women easy to sleep with in Nightindale'. Boom, it had 350,000 results. Seriously if even half of this number were easy to sleep with, this act was so done. He started browsing and there were few Escort services, Massage Parlor services, and few crazy articles, and few shady bars, again some Escort services, then lots of Escort services, and the list went on. God, this was not helping. He opened few of the articles that had list of clubs where finding girls easy to sleep with was easy.

Hell there were lots of them. Okay, this was a good head start. Max took a note of few of them, thinking that clubs would be nice place to get started. I mean girls in there didn't mind hookups, and flings, especially after a tank of booze. Max also felt like calling Jose his younger brother, as he must know where to find such girls, not because he was that type, but he was a boy who knew about things, all things, but Max's head said a big no. Max had to do this all by himself. He noted 5 of the shadiest bars, and now the wait started for night to dawn. Meanwhile, Max had played some video, on how to get a woman sleep with in a night. The videos went like this.

"Grab girl's back, and squeeze it hard. It is a clear signal, that you want her meat.".

"If she is feeling shy to show how badly she wants to sleep with you. Spill the drink in her cleavage. Make it clear, that you want those booties. It will ease her a bit.".

"When it's time to ask out, order a drink, first take a sip, then offer it to her. You will get the answer.".

"When she shows she is feeling tired, always flash the Hotel keys in front of her eyes. If you don't have a hotel key, flash your car keys. No women aren't dumb to think of it as hotel keys, and they know where you will drive her.".

"If she has put on lipstick more than 2 times in a night, think nothing to smash her lips with yours.".

Seriously, did all of this work. Max had never tried one of these, but tonight he needed all of them including a miracle to get laid with a woman to fuck her and not have sex. Max had no idea that grabbing n squeezing a woman's back could get her on bed. He had only seen men getting slapped for that. But tonight was a challenge, a challenge for Max to save her sister's dignity, and a challenge for manhood of Max if he was man enough to fuck a woman. The night had came in and Max was on his way to the dirtiest club of city named Pussy Cat. Of all the X Rated movies Max had seen in past, tonight it was all going to come in handy. Yeah, just getting in and just getting out, no kissing, no cuddling, Max though that would be enough to be qualified as Fuck.

But seriously, after doing this would he become a man, if it was so, then only the porn stars were men, who would fuck, yeah fuck a woman they didn't even knew. A part of Max didn't wanted to do this, but there was another part of Max which was curious on how Max would do it. Was Max actually excited for this night, as all men wanted was this. Hell no, was Max actually being driven crazy. Max cleared his head and there it was a long queue outside the club, with hell lot of girls and women. Max couldn't help but stare them one by one, as if he was picking his target for tonight. Max quickly parked the car and joined the crowd. A girl came in from behind.

Girl said, "Hey I feel you are looking for a partner. Would you be my date tonight.".

Max said, "Yeah, I am looking for a partner, because I can't fuck myself. I mean yes, we can date tonight.".

Girl smiled, "Oh you should learn to, and you will never have to date for that. Pervert.".

Clearly this was so not working, and how would it. I mean no dates, no lovely talks, no sweet promises for tomorrow, no kissing as if it was the last breath, and how would a man would expect a woman to get in his bed and be fucked for nothing good. I mean even if it was Brooce Willis, he would find to hard to get a woman in his bed by these terms. This try was totally gone, and so was the girl in the crowd. But Max couldn't have stopped, as time was running out. Probably this was the only night he had got. It has also been a long that Max hadn't used the art of indulging women, since he had met Stella. But seriously if only Stella had known what Max was doing in this shady club, she would so break up all ties with him.

There were cars flashing by his side as he was still in the crowd outside, and it was too risky to be spotted by someone known. So Max made a move, and paid double for a stag entry. There it was hordes of women, with that expression on their face, that hey who is going to be tonight. Max saw another woman who was dressed in shiny short dress, having drinks all by herself in a corner. She was staring couple of men, but neither of them came any closer, so Max did. Max reached for her, to grab her back to squeeze it hardest as he could.

The woman turned and said, “Oh that grab is really good. But with this you won’t even get my shit.”.

Wait, what, Max withdrew his hands, wiping on her dress, and got dissolved in the crowd, seriously and that man in that video never said anything about shit. But it did made sense, I mean grabbing a woman’s back had never made things easy. God this was so not helping. Despite of the fact that this club was full of women, Max was still hitting and trying. Seriously, this was the first time that Max was actually going crazy to get laid. The last time this happened must have been in previous life, because he couldn’t remember a thing. This was so not Max, and this was so not the type of man he was. Max’s eye fell on a distant corner, and he saw a couple getting cozy. There it was, Max just wanted a woman like that, and her sister’s tape would be safe.

Chapter 10

Will she be easy to sleep with, no, I mean look at her shoes, those are sneakers, and no doubt the first thing she would do after hearing Max's proposal was run. Not a good fit. Wait, will that be a good fit for tonight, no, no, she is having the same drink for last half an hour, she looks like a control freak, and loosing to a man would be something she wont prefer. God, why were all women looking like if they were from Venus. Not even one slutty woman with whom Max could have a stand off tonight. Max had his eyes all over the club, then a nice woman came by to sit beside Max. She smiled. Wait, that was a good signal. Max ordered few drinks for the lady which sure impressed her. Max took her drink, took a sip and then passed it to her.

The woman chuckled, "Oh so now I am safe, as this drink isn't poisoned. Feeling like a first Lady.".

Max said, "Oh no, no. That is a dirty gesture I saw online to tell women that a man wants to fuck her.".

The woman smiled, "Trust me that only happens online. So you better get a virtual cock too.".

She left, leaving Max hold his head. Why not, every woman would go away after listening that a man wants to fuck her. Max was now missing Jack n Jeff, seriously these both nuts would have helped a lot. But stakes were too high to get them involved. I mean no woman, after all those thousands of Google Search results. Max had always doubted and was now sure that this Google thing was all a fraud. I mean not even a single woman, though there were lots of single women on floor, but not even one who wants to get fucked. Come on, be it man or woman everyone likes to get laid, and getting fucked was just as same.

Seriously, this woman had got Max into some deep trouble. Of every thing, Max was sure if only this woman had told him to fuck her, Max would have enjoyed it the most, especially after everything that woman had made Max go through. But guess, she must have been saving that moment for some time later. Max swayed around the club trying to talk with few woman and getting straight to fuck. But all the woman gave him was a thumbs down. Of course this act too had to be difficult. Max didn't knew about fucking, but this woman was sure driving him crazy. Max knew that she must have been watching him, and enjoying every moment of it. Wait could it be Anna, as Max and Anna had too much sex when they were together, and maybe she was trying to avenge him for those memories. A woman bumped into Max, and there she was a perfect over drunk chick. Max got into a conversation with her. This time he was taking it slowly.

Max said, "That's it, I need to break it. I so want to fuck you, and I can't resist.".

The woman said, "Seriously. Everybody wants to fuck me, what's special about you, a golden cock maybe.".

Max said, "Well, I will say, that you better find out.".

The woman burped, "I will, someone who doesn't comes gold, in this mine of mine. You know the only gold women like is in rings, apart from that there is only this finger left for others.".

Seriously, now a woman was showing F off in sweetest way possible to Max. But she wasn't to be blamed, I mean such a nasty proposal didn't end up in getting thrashed was something Max was cherishing at the moment. God there has to be some way, Claudia's tape can't go on internet. What a dilemma it was, Max could not even tell a woman to sleep with her to save her sister's dignity. I mean all the normal women Max had known would do it very easily. The club was on verge of closing, and Max was not even an inch closer to his act of fucking a woman. All his options were running out. Yeah, I mean literally all the women of club were running out to their homes, or their boyfriends homes, while Max was just left with a drink in his hands. I mean come on, since when did Nightindale became a place hard to get laid in, of course only since that wretched woman had entered his life.

Max had even tried on the female bar tenders of the club, but again with a jerk off gesture. Max took his coat and strode out. Damn, now how would he save Claudia. Max went to the alley, and saw few hip girls having drinks in shade. Wait, Max could have tried on them. Max got his car parked beside them, while one of the punk girl stared at Max, and unbuttoned her jacket.

Whoa, that was some good signal. Max got out, and straight away pushed that girl on the wall. Tonight Max was so desperate to fuck someone that he would fuck this one right on this wall.

Max said, “Hey, let me get straight. I want to fuck you.”.

The girl said, “Of course you want to, as I see no holes in this wall behind.”.

Max pulled her jacket to throw it away and said, “Trust me, this wall is the best bed you will have around me.”.

The girl snapped back, “But what makes you so desperate, I am sure it isn’t me.”.

Max unzipped his pants and said, “If I don’t stop, after what I have got, will make me desperate.”.

Max had pulled down her skirt and the girl started screaming. Wait, she did started screaming like hell, with both of them half naked on street, while her couple of friends started bashing Max with a bag of trash. Seriously, this can’t be happening. Max didn’t cared, and went on pulling down her clothes. She screamed harder, and a police patrol car stopped by. The shit was getting real. Max had heard the siren, and he got down, while the girl kept screaming at Max, trying to gather sympathy from Policeman.

The girl said, “This man is freak. He tried to rape me. You scumbag.”.

The policeman said, “Hey are you okay. And you man, are you on drugs.”.

This was the most embarrassing moment Max was in. I mean first, he was not even bit attracted by that hip girl, and was still trying to fuck her. Second, it was first time any girl had accused him of raping. Third, Max was actually fucking a girl on street, like if it were 17th century French streets. God, either he could save his sister, or save himself. Max pulled over his pants. He realized that by clashing with this policeman and this girl would only worsen the situation, so he thought of making up to them.

Max said, “Hey I am sorry. I was drunk, and I am also a sex addict. I just lost my cool. No harm meant.”.

The policeman turned to the girl, “Hey, is this okay with you, or shall we head to the station.”.

Max said, “Trust me girl, I’ve been doing this a lot, lately. Do what others, simply walk away.”.

Max wasn’t sure, but it did worked exactly as he had thought. The girl got scared, so she took back her allegations, and they all moved back. Max accelerated his car to the top speed, to get the hell out of this shady nightlife area, before that girl changed her mind. Seriously, Max was this close to be arrested for an alleged rape. Seriously this was the last thing Max would have wanted to do, a Rape. God, this was like death of manhood. The last thing any man would want to get smudged in. Max was damning himself on what else was left to see. Why did he even came close to all those women in his life. Couldn’t it been that from the day he was born he had met Stella. I mean all this could have been avoided, but No, life had plans to screw Max. Wait, that wretched woman still had sex tape of Claudia. This wasn’t over. Max had to do something, some other woman, some other trick. Come on fucking a woman in Nightindale was like buying a burger, only if you had change.

Yes change it was, Max had to change his approach. None of those online tricks were working, so why not try it with a woman whom he was acquainted with but not familiar. That sounded good. If a woman from past can cause these trouble, then another woman from past could also fix these troubles. Wait there was one woman who always wanted to hook up with Max, get laid, and get fucked. Yeah, it was the friend of Stella, Maya. Maya always wanted to be with Max, and if now he said that he wanted to fuck her, Maya would undress herself first and then say a yes. Max got his car turned towards her house. She didn’t lived much far, and soon there was Max at her doorstep. She was little surprised to see Max at such odd hour, but they both got in. Max was sitting on couch and sipping to some exquisite wine.

Max said, “You know there is something about you that Stella can never have.”.

Maya flickered, “Oh, now you are telling me that you want that something, when you are this close to marrying one of my best friend. I hope it isn’t some, but a lot.”.

Max grabbed her by her back, “Hey, I want to fuck you. Isn’t it what you always wanted.”.

Maya smothered his cheeks, “I also wanted you to be with me. Anyways does Stella knows about this.”.

Max said, “Just leave her out of this. This night is about you and me.”.

Maya said, “Of course i will leave her out of this, we aren't having threesome. But what happens after you get to fuck me. I mean where does this goes.”.

Max said, “Once I have what I want, I will give you what you want. Again, again, and again.”.

That was how men do it, like a boss. But sadly it didn’t sound great for Maya, so next thing was Max again, standing at her doorstep biting his fists. Damn, Max had screwed his easiest chance of fucking a woman. I mean Maya always was so provocating and always sent wrong signals to Max, but why did she miss his proposal. Wait, hope Maya was not working with that woman. Max sat on her porch steps, holding his head. God, the time was running out, and at this odd hour Max would find no one to have a fuck with, apart from car thieves, and drug addicts, and they too would be men. Max thought that he should have said no word and maybe pounced on her. That would have worked, as here Max just got entangled in his own words. But anyways, Max had also missed an excellent opportunity to sleep with Maya, yeah she was one of the sexiest woman Max had come in contact with.

God, what was Max thinking, he was about to hit his fiancé’s friend. This was not so acceptable. But who cared, Stella had called off the wedding, and with this woman going crazy, this was so not ending soon. Wait could it be Molly, because Max still remembered the day he had refused to have sex with Molly when she had started undressing in his room. Maybe Molly was upset on how did Max refused her, and was taking her vengeance. Again, Again and Again, Max couldn’t believe that he actually said that. He very well knew that these again had come right from his heart. Wait, did he had lustrous intentions for Maya. Of course he did, the reason he was here at her doorstep. Max took the list out of dirtiest clubs from his pocket, as there were few that opened all night. His phone rang.

Stella said, “Max where are you, and don’t tell me that this woman of yours told you to fuck Maya.”.

Max exhaled, “Then what should I tell, that hey I had a boner this night, and couldn’t wait to get together with you.”.

Stella said, “Max this is not so cool. You just tried sleeping with my friend.”.

Max sapped back, “You know what else is not cool, that your friend almost bought it.”.

Stella said, “Max I don’t know what is happening to you. But don’t break my trust. This city is full of women that will say yes to sleep with you. But remember, next morning they will all be gone, but me. That’s all.”.

Max moaned, oh god why is this even happening. He hit his head with his cellphone. The next thing Max would never want was Stella saying those 3 magical words, Good Bye Max. But seriously this woman Maya was hell of a crook. In one night, Max had never wanted to fuck somebody as he did for Maya. She was trying to be a good friend to Stella, but had forgotten the means of friendship, every time she hit on him. Max’s phone rang.

The woman said, “Max, sometimes you are too good, but sometimes you are surprisingly disappointing. I clearly told you, that you have to fuck a woman whom you don’t know. And there you are at Maya’s doorstep. I hope you didn’t had a memory loss.”.

Max said, “I mean how can I. The only person that has lost their mind is you. And I don’t know Maya even a bit. I have just seen her twice or thrice.”.

The woman said, “You will have to try harder. So now you are not only fucking an unknown woman, but you will call me, and I will make you do some dirty things while you fuck. Trust me, these things are every man’s dream.”.

God, why did Max even thought about Maya. It was his fault, no it was his desires fault. Why did she even crept in his mind, and now this woman was going mad. Now how would he find such a woman who had no issues in getting fucked. I mean even Barbie doll would speak up to this. Damn Stella knew what Max was doing, and how would he justify this, by telling Stella that hey my sister is having a bang back at college. Why did even god created family, it was the strongest of support and weakest of link. There was Max hitting his leg on his car just outside Maya's house. Couldn't just world be a happy place, where Max and Stella and his family could live their rest of lives without being bothered. Few hours back Max was being accused of raping a girl, and he didn't knew what else will come upon if he tried those tactics again.

Wait, its all about the tactics, isn't it. I mean this woman behind the phone is playing games with Max, what if Max also played a game with her by her rules. Okay, that was making some sense. The first place that came to Max's head was Viceroy's Club. He was a member of it, and damn hell lot of women visited it. It was open all night, and Max would sure get someone to fuck by the rules. Max hurried up and got himself into the car. He drove as fast he could have. He even changed his dress into a suit that he always kept in his car for emergency meetings. This is how it was going to be, change in tactics. The club was all lit, as Max entered. He glanced his eyes over the club area and there were lot of women. Some young, some newly married, wait no chance, then some lonely angles too. His eye fell on a 35 something woman who was dressed in golden gown, with nobody around her. What was interesting was that she was staring at the dance area particularly to 40 something men who were dancing with their wives. That was it. Max rushed in to sit beside her.

Max said, "It is a sin to be alone when you are that beautiful. This sin is on them, but I can't be a part of it.".

The woman smiled, "Talking to strangers is also bad. Will bad work for you.".

Max said, "Oh, with that I assume, you want to stay stranger with me, Right. Miss.".

The woman said, “Miss Emily it is. And as I already told you, I don’t keep talking with strangers. Mr.”.

Finally something good was happening tonight. Wait this was good, not because Claudia’s sex tape was in question. But it was good, because Emily was a nice woman. Well not really nice, but she was sexy too. All this night Max had been hitting shady clubs that were popular for flings, but it was one of the best clubs of Nightindale where he finally found a match to fuck with. At least, with how things were going Max believed that this one will sure turn out well. They talked about each other, and Max even took her to the dancing floor to shake a leg or two. Yes shake a leg, not break a leg. It was Max who could clearly see on how happy Emily was to dance amidst those couple. Max was feeling guilty about his intentions, but Man this has to be this way. They drank, while Emily got much closer to Max. For a minute Max had even fantasized Emily. For Max she was so feeling like Stella, the reason Max was finding it more interesting to talk with her. It felt like that Emily had been sent by god to this club only for Max. But wait, Max was not going to move in to her house, it was all part of the game that wretched woman was playing. The dinner got on table, and they were slowly having a bite along with words.

Max said, “You know, it’s not with all women that I feel this close.”.

Emily said, “Really because I think men usually not consider this distance to be close. I mean, ha, I am also feeling quite close to you. But I have seen this a lot. Oh the dinner is about to be over. Wine?”.

Max said, “You are not getting it, It’s not the wine that I want. They sell those in supermarkets too.”.

Emily said, “So you mean that they shouldn’t. But then dinners would become so boring.”.

Max took a ring out of his pocket and said, “For last 3 years I have been carrying this ring, and I want to give this to the woman whom I am going to fuck. Because it will be the first and last time I am going to fuck anybody. I mean, fuck is such a gross word, but that is how this ring will reach the right person.”.

Emily got up from chair, while Max got shivers that in such a decent place he was going to get slapped. Emily sat on his legs, and kissed the hardest to Max that Max had ever experienced.

Chapter 11

It worked like a charm. Max didn't proposed anybody, and he made it clear that he wants to fuck the woman, and Emily just bought it. Change in tactics had worked. I mean for a minute Max thought that he was smarter, he was more clever than that online tip giving man. Whoa, this ring had just save Max's family from a huge embarrassment. Wait, it might have been too early but then things were looking in good shape. It turned out that Emily was a platinum member of the club that also had access to the guest rooms. So they were headed there. Emily also revealed that it had been 10 years that she had slept with somebody, while the way Max said about the ring was one of the manliest thing Emily had ever experienced. Seriously, was that Manly, Max couldn't believe.

Since the day this woman, not Emily, but that wretched woman has came in his life, Max had got to know many manly things that he never knew even existed. But seriously, the last thing that Max wanted was this Emily chasing him for marriage after this was over. I mean women were always over sticky and Emily was in mid 30's, and she would create lot of fuss after this. But seriously who cared, maybe she will understand, that everybody gets fucked. Wait whoa, they had just reached the guest room and Emily started undressing. There she was, one of the best things Max had seen lately, I mean the body of Emily. Despite of her age, she was a good competition to Stella. She pushed Max on bed.

Emily said, "Being strangers to being in bed. I feel that all our years have been so wasted.".

Max said, "Oh talking about time is such a waste, when it tells everything about itself in time.".

Emily felt a little confused, while Max pounced on her. The great unknown woman fuck had started. After few minutes of some censored action, Max took out his phone, and slowly placed the blue tooth ear piece in its place. He made the call to that woman, while he got cozy with Emily.

Woman said, “Now you will shove your cock in her back. Do it like an animal.”. God this was gross, but Max did it, while he could clearly see a little hesitation on Emily’s face. Seriously for a minute Max felt like placing the bed sheet on her face. I mean how could Max do this X Rated thing. But he did.

Woman said, “Slap on her face, grip her neck, while you do so.”. God this was the definition of a man in that woman’s dictionary. This was so not manly. But Max did it, while he saw Emily actually saying nothing.

Woman said, “Slap your hardest on her butt. I want to hear her moan.”. This was not so gross, but still slapping a woman while she had already agreed to sleep with you. Was this punishment, But Max did it.

Woman said, “Pull her hairs, to the max, while you shove your thing into her.”. I mean did this woman only knew about violent version of men. God, Max did it, while Emily couldn’t help but moan.

Woman said, “Now spit on her, keep spitting, every time your thing makes a move.”. Was she even real, I mean spit on her. To ease the comfort of Emily, Max opened her mouth with his hands to spit in it. While Emily was little confused on what was Max trying to do. Was it some Voodoo sex act.

The wretched woman told Max few other couple of dirty things that Max had never imagined that they even existed. But Max did it quietly. In all of this, Max some how felt good. I mean this was how every man wanted to do, over come his female partner. Did he just did something manly, wait, if a feminist was to be asked, Max would he hanged to death, but if a male X rated movie star was to be asked, Max would be a true bro. The only thing Max had wanted was Emily not feeling bad about it, as she had just saved Max and his sister too. But on the contrary, Emily was actually enjoying it.

Did this gap of 10 years made her desperate, or she had forgotten how things worked when people had sex. But wait, this was not sex, it was fuck, pure fuck. Max continued doing it, till he finally came, and the last thing that wretched woman wanted Max to do was, come thrice. And Max did exactly like she wanted, feeling this close to die of having that level of adrenalin rush. But Max did it, like men do, like tough men do, never give up. It was over, and Max lying on top of Emily, with head between her breasts. He woke up in a jolt.

Emily said, "Oh man, never been fucked like that. In fact, now I know what it means to be fucked. But I loved it.".

Max panted, "I loved it too. Emily you have no idea, but we both were getting fucked.".

Emily draped herself with bed sheet, "I am glad that you felt fucked too. Hey but where are you going.".

Max didn't say a word, and what would he say, that what he wanted he had got. Max strode out, while Emily was still in his head. Damn she was a nice woman, and seriously what Max did to her wasn't even a bit nice. Max took his phone out, again played the sample sex tape of his sister. Before the video played entire length, Max deleted it. Seriously, Claudia had no idea that his brother had just save her life. Yeah, it was no less than a life saver. After all with a sex tape on internet, social distress was as good as death. Max had proved to be a good son by saving his father, and now a good brother by saving his sister. Maybe someday when he would grow old, he would sure tell Claudia, what he had to do to cover up her mess. It felt for a moment that brothers were made to cover up for their sisters. This fuck a woman act was so done.

Max rushed in his car, and drove straight back home. It was early morning, but still the bed was calling Max. He fell on his bed, and woke with a jolt as if Emily was still under his body. God, now was this Emily going to haunt him, I mean the fuck was really horrible though they enjoyed. Max couldn't sleep well, the pretty face of Emily, then Stella in angst, then Daisy with questions, then Claudia with her boyfriend, then Max with broken leg, and of course, Nina, Nova, Anna, Aspen were all haunting him back. Max skipped his office and called Jay, Jack to his house. They were seated.

Max said, "What are you doing Jay, it has been days and we are no closer. We need to find her.".

Jack interrupted, "And what are you doing Max, simply following everything she says.".

Max snapped back, "It is because I listened that you are free to walk.".

Jay said, "Hey calm down everybody. Max we are close, we have many leads at this moment.".

Max said, "Seriously, yeah we do have leads, against all the women from my past. Do you call this progress?".

Jack interrupted, "Okay, okay. Now I get it. That woman made you do something else, that too within these couple of days when you were gone. Now I say that this is some progress, that you aren't telling us.".

Max said, "Yeah, Jay, I need you to put some man after a boy named Philip from Williamson University. He might not be a woman from my past, but I doubt he has something to do with this. Just keep an eye.".

Jay called one of his associate from Williamtown where the university was, to keep an eye on Philip, while Max felt a little insecure. Max thought to take his words back, as her sister could also come up. But anyways, no one would know about that tape, it would be so gone by now. But the point was that they still needed to find that woman. Jay had been busy with some other work, and today they were again going to hit the road and follow up with the leads. This was the part that Max hated most, following up on women he didn't even wanted to see again. Jack tried his best to get Max talking about what had happened in last day, but Max did it like a man, and avoided. Even Jay had got suspicious, about Max hiding something, but he didn't showed it, till he was getting paid.

Max had a friend in Alpha AI, in fact the man who was instrumental behind meet up of Max and Alpha AI founders. Now the plan was that Jay and Max were going to get everything out from this lead about Nova. They were driving to Alpha AI office, while Max couldn't believe that a dispute from 2 generations ago was now settling its score. I mean seriously, Nova was daughter in law to this family. I mean she wasn't born to Smith family, but still carried the rage against Max. What was wrong with people. I mean there were 6 more families like that of Max, weren't they on radar of Nova. Times have passed and Max's family was now capable enough to have a shelter in this city by their own. If it was Nova, then Max had made up his mind that he would give away their ancestral home, and bring his parents to his house. This was best a righteous man could do. They have reached Alpha AI office and on desk of Martin.

Max said looking back at Jay, "We might be on 4th floor, but this cubicle is the building block of Alpha AI.".

Martin said, "And this Man, i mean Max, is the lift that keeps us up.".

They laughed while Jay interrupted with a picture in his hands, "Hey, I need to break something quick. Have you seen this woman in the picture. We believe she has close ties with Alpha AI, and knows many things about you people. Nothing to be alarmed about, but we need to check few things.".

Martin took the picture and hit it on his other hand, "Yeah she is Nova. I know her, in fact I am the one who is finalizing her contract with Alpha AI.".

Jay said, "She is a housewife Martin, I mean what contract could she get into.".

Martin said, "Not just a housewife, but a fine one, who is making up for her house. Our founder knows Nova from long, and in recent times she was going through lot of financial troubles. So our founder suggested that she made use of her house skills, particularly cooking skills, and take up the catering contract of our office. This is how she gets into the picture, ah an appetizing picture.".

Max looked at Jay, and Jay looked at Max. "Oh, and we thought there was something else cooking here.".

A catering contract, I mean seriously. This was what she was coming here for, a catering contract. I mean woman with such financial distress would never be able to manage 30K dollars, so was Nova out of question. The circumstances said so, and plus she was a housewife, no, a housewife who was in contract with Alpha AI. God but why did she lied about not knowing what circumcision when she had got her son the same. This was no fitting well, but one thing was sure that Nova would not get into a catering contract only to cover the her real intentions of gaming up Max, but she was in financial distress. A woman in financial crisis can never afford satellite phones, that too, that many different numbers.

Max too was convinced that Nova might be innocent. Now they were headed to the community college where Ember's sister was studying. The plan was to confront her and maybe get some version of Ember's relationship with Diddy. As per Max Ember's sister, Lucy was too good to be a part of it. She was young, bold, and honest and would end up telling Max everything he wanted to know. Of course contacting Diddy was useless unless Max wanted to get in a dirty fight with him, so the only option they had was Lucy. Also as Max still remembered, Lucy was still in touch with Jose, as she still loved her, and answering Jose's elder brother's few question was just a good opportunity of rep building. But seriously Ember was just opposite to what Lucy was, she was a sharp edged knife without a handle, by all means. For Ember, Jose was still a villain who took undue advantage of Lucy. They had reached the college, and waited for Lucy to come out. There she was, talking to a bunch of her classmates. She noticed Max and came closer.

Lucy said, "Hi Max, its nice to see you again. Did Jose sent you, is he there in car.".

Max said, "I had no idea that you still liked me, I mean after Jose broke up. But seriously, would you find it nice to see me again, I mean feel nice if I be around in good shape.".

Lucy said, "Max, its always nice to see you, but once in while. I Mean don't just stay around me. Kidding.".

Jay said, "Oh I go that. Hey Lucy I wanted to ask you what's between Ember and Diddy.".

Lucy exhaled, "Argh. I am tired of telling everybody about what my sister is doing with that crook. The thing is that I am dating Diddy's brother, but wait he is a nice man and not a hoodlum. We both are pretty serious. So my sister is getting close to Diddy, so we could get together forever. But Hey Max, it will still be nice to see you.".

Jay said, “You are saying that your sister is dating a man, so his brother keeps dating you.”.

Lucy said, “I know I am a teenager, but I can’t keep dating somebody for life. Getting it.”.

Max looked at Jay, while Jay looked at Max. Seriously one thing was out of question that Ember didn’t made up with Diddy so Max could get beaten. She had her reasons, actually well satisfying reasons. This was just another family watching the back of their own ones. In fact Ember was just like Max. On the first instance she had fought with Max because of her sister, and here she was compromising with herself so her sister could get settled well. Damn she was a nice woman. But wait, Max wasn’t on crusade of finding women like him, but he had to find that wretched woman. But then why did she lied that she was looking for a man for Lucy. I mean Lucy was seeing a man already. Was it because Ember didn’t liked Lucy getting married into a family of hoodlums. Of course any decent woman wouldn’t like that, but wait was Ember decent, no she wasn’t, especially all the foul words she had thrown on Max when Jose had broken up with Lucy. But anyways, this lead too was turning up dead.

There was nothing solid that could prove that Ember was that woman. Of everything, not all women from Max’s past were twisted bitches. Now Molly was the next lead, Jay wanted to catch up with. Parking the car by her house was no good, as she barely came out, so they were now headed to organ donor bank, the same org. that had sent Molly that letter. Molly’s case was interesting, and one of most dubious too. After all if only Max had listened to his parents, he would be with Molly not Stella. Molly had the best motive. Max thought, seriously could Molly do things like this to hurt Max. Of course she could, I mean she couldn’t be trusted. The fact that after Max, Molly hadn’t seen any man was quite alarming that she hadn’t still moved on. Jay and Max were in the organ donor bank talking to an officer.

Jay said, “Why is it called Organ Bank. I mean if I donate a kidney, will it become two in 5 years.”.

Officer said, “It won’t become 2, but we are bank because we have 2 many of them.”.

Jay said, “Okay what if I want to leave my kidney for my generations to come.”.

Officer said, “We are an organ bank, so we keep organs, not fossils.”.

Max interrupted by showing him a picture, “Hey we got your piece of mind, I mean not brain, but what you are saying. We just wanted to check if you know this woman. By knowing doesn’t means that if you have dated her, but anything that you might recall about her coming here.”.

Officer said, “Yeah, she is Molly. I know her, of course she didn’t donated us her heart. But she was here looking for a liver, and one more woman accompanied her who would sit there in lobby, while Molly did all talking.”.

Max looked at Jay, while Jay looked at Max. Jay took Max’s phone and showed her a picture. Officer said, “Yes she is the woman. Hey but wait, I hope you aren’t police and they aren’t bank robbers. Ha”.

Jay said, “Max please return him the piece of mind, you got. I think he needs it.”.

Max didn’t say a word and they both got back in the car. By the way that picture on phone was of Daisy. So apparently Daisy was with Molly when she visited this organ donor bank. Whoa, this was strange, as Daisy should have done this with some family member, and not an ex of Max. But one thing was sure that Daisy and Molly were still close friends, even after everything happened. But Daisy never mentioned it that she was meeting Molly. What could be the reason. I mean if everything was to be normal, Daisy should have visited the organ donor bank with Stella, and not Molly. This was strange. And why was Molly showing such interest in Max’s family, when she knew that they will never get together. But seriously one thing was sure that chances were odd that Molly was that woman, because she was just helping Max’s family in getting that organ for his father.

God, so this was another dead end, that probably Molly had nothing to do with circumcision, or fuck an unknown woman. In fact, Molly had again crept inside Max’s hearts soft corner. Wait, he was not again getting together with Molly. So now it was

Nina, whom they had to tail, the pseudo police officer who was seeing a real police officer. The childhood crush, who couldn't get over Max. You know being a man always meant that there were some women in your life. But seriously, women like these who make your life hell, would make a man wish that he weren't even a man. Nina had her reasons, she was always avoided, neglected, by Max, and maybe now was trying to have complete attention of him. Maybe she didn't liked Max being too man to neglect a crush, and was now testing on how man he really was. Seriously, was it that bad to be a man. Jay and Max had now entered the regional police office where Jay still were friends with few officers. Their plan was to get info. About what Victor was up to.

Chapter 12

Jay said, "A lot has changed, since the last time I was here.".

Officer Wilson said, "Of course it has Jay. Nothing is permanent, not you, not me, not this place.".

Jay said, "Hey, hey, you think I couldn't be a permanent guy in this office.".

Officer Wilson said, "Oh I take back my words, because some things just don't change.".

Max interrupted before Jay could reply, "Hey guys, change of topic to something more important, because I can't see my life being changed like that. Hey Wilson, we need some intel from you. Do you know anything about Victor, the senior officer in Public surveillance team. I mean what all he is watching these days, whom is he meeting, and what is he up to. Any change, I mean any deviation in him from his regulars.".

Wilson said, "Victor is a nice chap, a very helpful guy who will go out of his way to help others. Recently he is been assisting Nina, a girl from neighborhood. Her uncle's shop got robbed recently, and Victor is helping her get all the surveillance tapes about that robbery so her uncle could get the insurance money. Apart from that, his routine is regular, he comes in time, and goes out in time. I can introduce you to his nearest colleagues, if you want.".

Max said, "That won't be needed, I think you have changed my thoughts about Victor.".

So this guy Victor was not keeping an eye on Max, but instead he was helping Nina's uncle get the insurance claim. Max looked at Jay, while Jay looked at Max, and they both looked the other way. Max thought, what if Nina was mad at him for not being a couple, but still she was good at heart, and she would never do such things to Max. Actually it was stupid to think that way. All this time Max thought that Nina was trying to keep an eye on Max with help of Victor, but it was her uncle whom she was helping.. Max should have known it. But wait, why on that day, Victor acted like if Nina was her girlfriend, I mean he did gave lots of bad vibes. Maybe he was overprotective of Nina.

Anyways, that was good for Nina, that she had finally found a man who liked her too. Well seriously both of them would look good too, but then who was this woman who trying to make things difficult for Max.

It wasn't Molly, it wasn't Nova, it wasn't Ember, it wasn't Nina. So was it Aspen, if so they would very soon get to know about it, as now they were headed to tail Aspen. Seriously a woman whose dream got shattered by Max could be a great reason to avenge back. I mean she had lied about Platterina, and why in the world would a woman lie about going to a restaurant. Also Nina had some deep rooted relationship with people at Platterina, so she could have easily pulled that fight off. The plan was that Jay and Max were going to meet Oscar, yeah he would be mad on meeting Max who fired him, but then only he could tell, if his getting the job at her firm was a co incidence or a pre-planned act. They had reached Aspen's office, and it was evening, while Jay n Max waited for Oscar to head out. There he was.

Max said, "Hey Oscar, good to see you rolling again. Congrats on the new job.".

Oscar frowned, "But it's not nice to see you. By the way, this new job is only because I was fired from old one.".

Max said, "I am sorry, really I am. But please know that I didn't hate you. You were just misfit.".

Oscar snapped back, "Oh you know what didn't fit, your hatred in my relieving letter. Huh".

Jay interrupted, "Hey cool everybody, we are not firing up things again. Hey Oscar, I know Max is little wreck, but remember the good times with him. He needs your help right now. We just want to know, how did you got the job here, and if you knew Aspen from before. Or if Aspen helped you secure a job here. And also know, that we don't have malicious eyes on your new job, but we are happy to see you do good.".

Oscar said, "It was an online Job advert I saw, and I applied. Luckily I was able to explain my recruiter that my ex reporting manager hated me, and we never had a good time, to which she believed and offered me this job. And Aspen, you mean the receptionist, I didn't knew her from before. And trust me, in here everybody is able enough to only secure their jobs, no way Aspen could have helped to get me placed here.".

Jay looked at Max, "Is internet a woman, because it helped Oscar for this job.".

Of course internet was not a woman nor was internet after Max's back. Seriously it was hard to digest that Aspen didn't knew Oscar, but it was the truth. So two of Max's enemy didn't knew each other, but were working at the same place. Max didn't knew if it was a good news or a bad news. Good news because Aspen had no grudges against him, bad news because someone else than Aspen did and these both didn't knew who. But it also made sense, I mean Max had just got her company shut, while life was much more than that, but then this wretched woman also had just got Max circumcised, break a leg, fuck a woman, and fire a colleague. Well the equation was same. But after the conversation with Oscar, getting his job here seemed such a coincidence. Maybe just because Max had hired a detective, everything was appearing to be suspicious.

Max held his breath while they were sitting in the basement of office in their car. Jay was busy connecting his phone with the phone software he had. He was up to something nasty. The last of lead was Anna, and of all what has happened, she was supposed to be that woman. Max's head was now shifted to Anna, I mean all those good times didn't meant anything to her. She was out with rage on Max. She had to be that woman. God was dumping a girlfriend such a grave crime, I mean what was wrong if Max had found another one in Stella. This woman Anna had some serious issues with herself. Jay was done with his software and he hit the button enter to make a call to Anna coming from no of Tax Fraud Department.

Jay said, "Hey this is Jason from Tax Fraud Dept. and I'm not calling you to award Best Tax Paying citizen.".

Anna said, "Of course I know, because I'd not nominate myself for such award even if it was free.".

Jay said, "Hey don't act smart, you have violated federal laws.".

Anna said, “Seriously, because that was not on my bucket list.”.

Jay with other hand forwarded her a forged mail and said, “I believe neither was going to Jail. Just check your mailbox. There will be an intermediary document that we are going to file in court, because you have just made 50K dollars disappear from your tax filings. Yeah we have caught the hole in your accounts Miss Anna. So we are soon going to see you in court of law while we sue you.”.

Anna stammered, “Hey, hey, hey I am sorry. I was just trying to be hard nut. Wait, I can explain that. These 50K dollars I liquefied, were given to Bad Tony from Vegas. See he is a goon and a casino owner, much the same thing. My boyfriend played few poker games on credit, and there we fell in his trap. If I hadn’t given that money, this Bad Tony threatened to cut my boyfriends thing. I mean what would I do of him without it. For proof I have replied with a bank transfer statement. Please leave us out of this.”.

The transfer statements were true, and Jay hanged up the phone. “I can sure bet on this.”.

Again there was silence in the car. Max was silent, because he was mad, really mad, because nothing good was happening to catch or to even stop that woman. Jay was silent because he was embarrassed for not being able to catch that woman, while all his leads were turning up dead. Seriously what kind of investigation was this, all six suspect coming out clean, as if this woman was a ghost. Not even Anna. Then who the hell was she. Max had always been good to others, and this was what he deserved, someone out of nowhere haunting his days and nights. And seriously Anna paid a thug only to save the thing of her boyfriend, because what would she do without it. God, what had Anna become World Bank of Men, rescuing troubled men. Maybe Max should also approach her, and maybe Anna would do something to save him, because clearly this Jay was no good.

I mean what had they had done till now, apart from being stunned by the goodness of these women. Of all things, this wretched woman had proved her cleverness over Jay, the retired

Police officer, or precisely a fired police officer. Max knew that this was not over, and this woman now would do something nastier, while Max's life was going to become even worse. Seriously, now Max realized how helpless Oscar must have felt when Max fired him. I mean for the first time in life Max didn't knew what to do. He was never like that, he knew he had to talk to Stella when he saw her for the first time, he knew he had to become an investment banker, he knew he had to buy his own house by the age of 27, he knew them all, and he did them well. But now was never like before, Max had no clue what to do. He entered his house along with Jay. Wait the lights were turned on, who could be it. Max thought, oh no, not now.

Daisy said, "Max this is unbelievable, last night you went to sleep with Maya, oh to fuck her.".

Jay interrupted, "Seriously this is what you think is important, I don't wonder why women are after you.".

Max held his head and said to Jay, "Hey, she was my wives friend, okay.".

Daisy snapped back, "Of course fucking wives friend is not at all important, it's a normal thing, right Max.".

And there was Jack, "You are right Daisy, wives friend, friends wife. Thank god I'm not married.".

Max said, "Hey all of you, stop it. I was little drunk, and I thought that maybe I will find Stella at Maya's place. You know she always visits her when she is upset. So I went there, and I met Maya. I met Maya, and things got little cozy. As I said I was drunk, so I mistook Maya to be Stella, and I asked her to get fucked, I mean sleep with me. But then I got back into consciousness, and I even strode out. That was it.".

Daisy calmly said, "Oh now you have a legit excuse of visiting Maya again, because Stella is so upset right now.".

Jack said, "Yeah, even I am upset, where does this Maya lives.".

Max stared back at Jack gesturing that he was so dead. Max turned to Daisy and said, "Hey Daisy, I hope you are done, so why don't you tell us now about your friendship with Molly. I though our family was done with that chapter, so why are you still hanging up with her now. Daisy, its important, yeah really it is.".

Daisy said, "She is a friend Max, and I don't need to tell you all about my friends. Maybe because now I don't want Molly to tell people that hey Max wanted to fuck me too. Do what ever you want.".

Daisy strode out, while all three men stood looking at each other. Obviously as soon as Daisy had left, Jay and Jack were again on Max's side, patting his back, calming him down. Seriously, were friends supposed to be like these. God save everybody from friends. Max fell on his couch, thinking what a witch Maya was. Stella was already mad at him, and now he fought with his dearest sister Daisy. God, all the women from his life were turning up against him. Seriously, what a man Max had become. Definitely a man not loved much, though he still had his place in Jay's, Jack's, Jeff's heart, but guess that was not enough. All this world talked about women equality, but only if they had known that one woman can create that much of trouble, they would have taken back their words. I mean just one woman had turned Max's life upside down. He was now a villain to all the women he had always tried keeping happy.

Stella was against him, Daisy was against him, and probably if he went back to his parental home he would find a lecture or two by his mom too, All of this, just because of one woman. Max never hated any woman, but now things had changed, there was one enemy in Max's life and that was this woman behind those satellite numbers. Max was not going to stay quiet, even if that woman was done. This woman needed to be caught. A phone bell rang, and again Max, his hands, and his heads were together. Jay raised, and gestured his phone which was ringing. Seriously now Max had this new phobia against phone bells.

Jay said, "Hey Max. The boy Philip you told about, we have everything about him.".

Max said, "Good to know, that you are still good with men. Anyways tell me about it.".

Jay said, "This boy Phillip, studies in Williamson University. He is a marketing grad, and a total cock. All he knows is being around girls, and sting them when the time is right. By now, as the moment we speak in, he had slept with more than 15 girls. In fact he has a website where this score is displayed. In short, if someone was to make him meet your wretched woman, his score will only turn 16, and nothing else about him.".

Jack interrupted, "Hey Max, isn't this same university where Claudia your sister is studying. I think we should also warn her about him. Such a monster.".

Max irritatingly said, "Thanks for concern Jack. But she is quite net savvy and must have seen that counter.".

Jay said, "Hey Max, everything isn't on internet. I think you should talk to your sister.".

Max said, "Hey, its okay. I already had a word with her. She is safe and has a boyfriend who takes care of her. Also she is not going anywhere on internet, so she won't be intimated. And now Jay lets get on point, what do we do about these 6 wicked women. They all can't be clean, or else you have chosen the wrong ladies. Trust me Jay she is going to call again and make me do something evil which I just don't want to.".

Jack said, "Yeah I agree. And Jay you should've taken my help while choosing ladies.".

Jay said, "We are humans Jack, we can commit mistakes, even god does it too, like when he made you a man. And Max, trust me, in all of my career if I have honed anything, then it's my instincts. And they tell me that something is wrong with these 6 women, also that they are closest to harm you. I know we don't have anything solid, so its time to confront them. Yeah, now you are going to meet them 1 by 1, apologize for the past, and try to be friends. This has 3 advantages. The woman might panic and do something wrong. The woman can also forgive you, which will end this. Or the last that unknowingly she will reveal herself and we will catch her.".

Max sighed, "Do you think this will work.".

Jack said, "Like if anything else had been working. I mean, I am with Jay.".

You know what people like most, running from their past. And now Max had to confront it. All these 6 women had been out of touch with Max, and Max hadn't bothered to drop a hello, or a birthday card. But now he had to meet them. I mean all the awkwardness of this world at the same time. Jay had said, that this was the last time they were trying on these 6 women, even if now it didn't worked, they would switch on alternative energy, I mean alternative strategy on rest of the women. Max had never imagined that he would be meeting them again, but that is what we humans call fate. It was fate that had got them together, again. It sounded weird, as Max had to apologize to these women, despite of the fact that Max himself had done no wrong to them. But then this was what we humans called save your back. It was highly impractical to be friends again with people whom you were on bitter terms. But then it was what we humans called, contingency plan.

The plan was simple that Jay would accompany Max, while they will follow these women 1 by 1, and bump into them accidently, where Max would express all his feelings, while Jay would just observe their reaction. It looked pretty simple, unless one of them reacts to slap Max, which Jay had warned, as all were quite hot up in head. The first woman they were going to meet was Nova. Max had insisted that they all met in a place where these women be most decent. So they had followed Nova up to Alpha AI office. She was just entering inside, while these both were behind. Max called out her name. So here was the face off.

Max said, "Hey Nova, it's so nice to see you again. How you been doing?".

Nova blankly said, "Of course it must be nice, in fact good, to see the person whose house is now yours.".

Max said, "Really Nova, you know we still have that painting of your forefathers in our living room.".

Nova said, "Everybody likes to have a renaissance era painting in their living room. By the way do you still tell the visitors of house that it is your forefathers.".

Jay said, "I bet he does, because renaissance era forefathers is also cool.".

Max exhaled, "Nova, now as we have met, there is something I want to say. I am sorry, my family is sorry, I am sorry on behalf of my great grandfather. You know what I have been thinking of naming that house back to you. I really am. Can't we be friends, and smile at each other when we meet. Love looks good as a legacy, not hatred.".

Chapter 13

Nova smiled, "You know what Max, I am not mad at you, neither at your great grandfather, because shit like this happens with everybody. We have to deal with seeing someone else's house that belonged to us, while you have tell your house visitors some man hanging in your living room as your forefather. You know, everybody gets what they deserve, which means maybe your grandfather deserved that house, and maybe that I deserve it back. As I said, I am not mad at you, because I don't like insensible things. But you got to live with this legacy of hatred.".

Max said, "Come on Nova. Think about your kids, do they need live with hatred of a lost house, or do they deserve love of a neighbor like me. Yeah, I want to get past that.".

Nova smiled, "Max are you okay, because I am not buying my own house from you. Now let me pass too.".

Nova left while jay kept watching her. "Seriously, are you giving back the house.".

Max whiffed, "My dad would not even let that painting go. Now all of it is a family.".

Max hadn't expected any wonder to happen, and it went exactly like it was supposed to. But of all, Nova felt very normal, like if she had forgotten Max, or maybe Max was just in her mind few minutes before. This was an either kind of situation. But clearly she didn't gave a damn about that house, most probably because she had moved on, was happy with what she got, and was busy in her day to day life. It also felt like if she was over Max, and his family too. So grudge was nowhere around Nova. Was she innocent, this was too early to say, unless Max and Jay had met other women too. But one thing did struck Jay, when she said that shit like this happens with everybody. I mean if Max would have told her about what all was happening in his life, she would have said the same. This was little dubious.

Another thing that bothered Jay was that Nova didn't accepted Max's friendship. I mean her parting words, were just let me pass too. On the other hand, Max was really thinking of talking to his dad about their parental house. I mean seriously with grave financial burdens, he would only help a woman, and be better blessed. Now the next woman they were going to tail was Ember, the protective sister. She was one hot piece, I mean one had to be beware of what she could do, especially with a man like Diddy behind her. They had decided that they won't meet Ember in her house, but at the café where she worked. It was a perfect place to catch up with an old enemy over a cup of coffee. The whole point of confronting these women was to calm them down, and any argument specifically with 'the one' could have worsen things. They both entered the café and sat on a table, while Jay spotted Ember coming towards them. Both were holding back to their nerves.

Ember said, "What can I get for you Max, apart from your favorite, the poison.".

Max turned back, "Hey Ember, its so nice to see you, how have you been doing.".

Ember said, "If you are feeling nice to see me, then I must be doing well. Order please.".

Max said, "Come on, I can't order you anything. I mean not now. Has anyone told you, that you look even more beautiful when you have that angst on your face. And yes recently I saw Lucy. God she still looks so pretty.".

Ember smiled, "Seriously, because I'm not sure, if your brother is still same as cock sucker as before.".

Max held her hand to make her sit beside him, "Ember, I am sorry, I am sorry on behalf of my brother. I know he is young, he is naïve, and irresponsible. But he is a good chap, just like me. He made a mistake, of not choosing your sister of course, but by letting her go. You know his biggest punishment is not having Lucy in his life. And one day he will realize it. I just didn't said much back then, because he is too young to understand. But seriously, why should we be enemies, just because of our siblings. You know we should go out some time.".

Ember said, "I don't know about we, but if you are not ordering anything, you probably will have to go out. And yes we are not enemies because of our siblings, but only because of your sibling. Okay.".

Max said, “Of course. My bad, I mean my brother Jose’s bad. Really.”.

Ember said, “Hey, stop being so nice. I know my sister is pretty, and many boys have taken an undue advantage of it. But guess what she has found her Mr. Right. So its all okay. Maybe you should forget all of this, forget Lucy, and especially forget me too, unless you choose to keep coming to my café. And I am just going to send couple of lemonades, so you can chill in these sour times.”.

Ember walked away, while Jay said, “How can someone forget her, seriously.”.

Ember had made it clear that she didn’t wanted to be friends with Max. Was it a great sign, no i mean she didn’t gave any positive sign. In fact, she couldn’t even stand seeing Max in her café. So could she stand talking to him, and making him do all these acts, of course she could. I mean she still hated Max’s brother and had assumed that Jose had taken undue advantage of her sister. This was enough as a motive. Also she clearly said that they still were enemies. In whole of this conversation Ember was against Max. This was really interesting. Jay couldn’t help but notice that the specialty of this café was shakes, but still she chose to send them lemonades. Ember, ember, ember, this woman was trying her best to act normal with Max, but deep inside she so wished choking Max to death. But again, this was too soon to hold a prejudice, as Jay suggested that Max met other women too, so next up was Molly.

The in house woman, the woman that probably hated sunshine, so obviously there must not have many things bright up in her head. Also now it was official that Molly and Daisy were still friends. They were chatting on Facebpad, they were meeting in real world too. But seriously, how could a woman who was rejected by a man for marriage be still friends with his sister. I mean women never were that way. So obviously, Molly still had hope in her heart that she could get together with Max, else why would such an introvert woman go to an organ donor bank and do all the talking. Molly did had some agenda, so Jay wanted to find it. As Molly would barely come out of her house, they decided to confront her in the nearby retail mart, where she went up everyday to buy food groceries. Max and Jay were just behind the shelf Molly was picking lettuce from. Max came around to bump into her.

Max said, “Hey Molly, it’s nice to see you. How have you been doing?”.

Molly said, “A man only finds nice to see his woman, and I am not your woman Max.”.

Max said, “Hey, hey. I had never wanted to be your man, but something more special, a friend.”.

Molly chuckled, “I don’t know about you, but I only had one friend, who left me to myself. Friends don’t do that Max. Friends don’t make excuses. And trust me, you can’t be friends with everyone.”

Jay interrupted, “I agree, this man had sent me a Facepad friend request even before we met.”.

Max held her hands, “Hey Molly, listen to me. I am sorry, I am sorry for what ever happened between us. I am sorry that I left you. I am sorry that I disappointed my family, I disappointed Daisy. Back then I thought, I liked Stella, I was attracted to her, still I am, I won’t lie. But I miss being with a friend when I am with Stella, you know why, because she cannot just take your place. You are still in my heart, and maybe one day I will realize what I have lost in you. I hope I not be too old then, to be not able to make up.”.

Molly smiled, “You know Max, you have lost me the day you rejected that marriage proposal. But I don’t hold any grudges, in fact what I still hold is the wedding dress I had got for us, and trust me, it will not be used in this lifetime, unless a miracle happens between us. I know where my place is, its in my own home. Well it can get little lonely sometimes, but I am happy as I am not surrounded by fake people. Of all the things, least I would want, will be your apology, because it doesn’t matters, and pity, which you are mistaken about.”.

Max exhaled, “Why is it to be like this between us. I really miss listening to your secrets in our attic.”.

Molly said, “I am sure that Stella too has many of them that you will enjoy.”.

Before Max could say anything else, Molly snapped back, “Lastly, I was here to buy my groceries, neither your thoughts, nor your apology. And now I am not letting anyone break my heart.”.

Molly strode out, while Jay said, “Did you got what you were here to buy?”.

Molly, Molly, Molly, this woman actually had a dormant volcano in her heart, waiting to be triggered by only one man, Max. I mean seriously, a 5th grader would also know, how much she still was into him. Forget 5th grader, even a mentally retarded man would see that Max was so running up in her head. Seriously, Jay was impressed, not with Molly, but the fact that Max had some serious fans. She actually called Stella, a fake person, and Max didn’t say a word. This was an eternal love story, and for a moment even Jay felt confused if Max was faking his love or was it true. The most funny thing of all that this woman Molly knew where her place was, in home. Seriously, it felt like if she enjoyed staying in home more than with Max. God, if this were happening in a film shoot, Molly would sure take up the Oscar. I mean she was good, to an extent that even Jay felt Max to be a culprit. But wait, that wasn’t the point, finding that woman was. I mean after this conversation one thing was sure that Molly didn’t wanted to be Max’s friend, no way. But deep in her heart, she would definitely want Max to marry her. I mean this was the most probable reason she was hanging out with Daisy. Second she didn’t liked much company, and it was evident that if she wanted to be with Max, it should have been only two of them, so it made sense that she was acting all alone. Also she was the only person who knew everything about Max’s family, inside and out. But again it was too early to judge that.

Now the next woman they were on tail for was Nina. Her uncle might have been robbed, but still she had a man who had access to all public eyes. By the way, her grudge was the oldest. She was also one of the women who had not seen any other man than Max, and her wait was the longest. Of all she was a well qualified suspect. Now confronting her could have been odd in her house, so Max and Jay decided to meet her in a local book reading club, where she went every day without absence. She was sitting even today too, and they approached.

Max said, "Hey Nina, it's so nice to see you, after that long. How have you been doing?".

Nina looked up, "Oh, its nice to see you too, but for the first time. And I don't tell strangers about my life.".

Max said, "Seriously, how can you forget your first crush, your only crush, the man of your high school dreams. Hey, it's me Max, back from the time when you had braces.".

Nina wowed, "Oh it's you. But seriously you got your facts wrong. It wasn't only you, I had a crush on.".

Jay interrupted, "Seriously, you had a crush on him. Now I don't wonder that you are a fiction reader.".

Max said, "Hey, Listen I might not be as interesting as that book you are reading, ah that's a crime mystery, and I might not be as good looking as I was once, but seriously I miss you looking at me like then. You know you were the only girl that made me feel like a hero, a stud, a prince charming. I mean seeing you here, brings all that back. I know you are mad at me, for not making you feel the same, and for that I am sorry, I am sorry for being a attention craver, I am sorry that I neglected you. But I will be happy if we can be friends.".

Nina placed her book down, "It's nice to have lovers, isn't it, also nicer to seeing people from your past. But you know what that you are wrong, when you say that you might not be as attractive as before, because nothing has changed, you are still so full of crap. And wait, you didn't neglected me, but you did a huge favor by getting my life ruined thinking more about you. So a huge thanks. And also let me tell you what I miss about my high school days, is having a pair of glasses along with those braces.".

Max placed his hands over her, "I know you are upset. It happens with people you care about.".

Nina withdrew her hands, "Oh you ignorant little Max, I knew why you didn't came to our reunion.".

Max coughed, “Hey, I was sick, I really was. Would you have liked me puking on our fellow mates.”.

Nina snapped back, “You are still so sick. I don’t know why you are here. But I am so upset, not at you, but at the fact that I won’t be able to finish this book today, because I am so done for now.”.

Nina strode away while Jay said slowly, “Thanks god her braces are gone, because she likes crime fiction.”.

Nina, Nina, Nina, can someone be so upset with somebody. She obviously didn’t say it, but it felt like she was screaming that hey you scumbag, you ruined my high school days. God, that much of rage, plus crime fiction on top of it, made her quite an eligible culprit. I mean this woman lied so clearly, that even the librarian of the book club was smiling when she strode out. She clearly avoided recognizing Max, when it was clear on her face that she did knew it. I mean with confronting of these women, Jay was becoming a fan of Max. I mean how could a man have that many lovely ladies in his life. Of all, she felt like disturbed. But it was uncertain to say, if she expected Max here, or was it totally out of blue. She was another woman who couldn’t stand a sight of Max. At least her rushing out of the book club indicated so. Her rage and Ember’s rage had something in common after all. But why did she lied on not recognizing Max. Maybe she was simply avoiding any encounters, or was she embarrassed. I mean if she wanted to ignore Max, why would she call him after every 2 3 days to do something manly. It didn’t made sense. If she wanted to ignore Max, and she was the woman doing it. Then her coming here was no brainer, because that woman had eyes on Max, so she would know that Max would meet her here, or was coming here. This was so not fitting well.

But anyways, now they had to move on, and tail Aspen, the woman with broken wings with Max behind her with arrows. I mean these acts that this woman was making Max do, were sort of deconstructing and damaging too, so a woman like Aspen whose life got ruined by Max, had enough reasons and motive. Max had broken her dreams, and maybe now Aspen was blurring Max’s reality. It made sense. But of all, she was the hardest to be friends with, because she didn't had any personal relationship with Max. They knew meeting in her office could create a scene, so they chose the parking lot of same office. She was heading towards her car and they appeared.

Max said, "Hey Aspen, it's nice to see you. How have you been doing?".

Aspen clichéd, "You know what's not nice, is getting people entangled in fraud lawsuits.".

Max said, "Come on Aspen, its over. You have a new job, and this one seems to be a new car. Isn't life good.".

Aspen said, "Oh yes life is good, if you think becoming a receptionist right from CEO is normal.".

Jay interrupted and said softly, "From a private cabin to a common lobby, ouch.".

Max said, "Hey look Aspen, this was nothing personal. I did what I felt was right then. You know me, and you know even how excited I was to bring you on board. In fact I advocated for you, with my bosses. You know why, because I believed in you and your skills. It just happened before I could realize that it will ruin your life. Every thing was going well, but then I felt cheated. And trust me, some day or the other, this truth was going to surface by some one or the other. Let's just get over it. I want to be friends with you, and maybe share a drink or two.".

Aspen flickered her eyes, "I know all of that Max, including that you are so professional. I mean you have an acumen of an investor, and intellect of a judge. Yeah that sounds impressive. I mean I wondered on why didn't the industry called you the watchdog of Investing firms. After all you have earned it. Seriously Max, do you think that by having fake educational documents can affect someone running a business. My startup was profitable, and god damn we were giving you good returns. But no, for the great idealistic Max.".

Max said, "Hey I am sorry, I really am. Seeing you upset makes me feel good, as I hope you will forgive me.".

Aspen snapped back, "Forgive you, but for what, you did the right thing, or didn't you.".

Max said, “That’s not cool Aspen, only if you could have seen things from my place.”.

Chapter 14

Aspen said, "I'd love to switch the places. So why not from tomorrow you sit in my lobby, and I will in your cabin. Ah but did that sounded unfair, oh yes, thought so. Good bye Max.".

Aspen got in her car while Jay said, "Oh places are so changed for being the watch dog.".

This woman had some serious issues, I mean why not, Max had got her from board room to greeting every other person. Aspen even didn't blink an eye while she saw Max, as if it was Max that she always thought about. Like if Max had never gone out of her memory. But wait the place that Max had in her memory was pretty despicable. Obviously she hated Max for everything he did. For her, fake educational documents was nothing and no crime, well that pretty much indicated that getting things done by a man like breaking a leg, firing a colleague would also be nothing for her. Of everything, she still had a connect with Max. But Jay was also disappointed that Max didn't told him that their relationship was more than a founder and an investor, I mean they had shared drinks before. This was quite like buddies did, and it didn't mattered if Max didn't considered her friend, but what if Aspen had emotions for him. As everyone knows that criminals are negative people, but what most don't know is that most of criminals are not satisfied with their life, and Aspen clearly didn't liked her life nor her job. I mean she was turning out to be a well qualified suspect. Jay had clearly sensed that Aspen had no regards for law, or what was righteous.

But anyways, time was to tell, while they were now going to tail Anna. The most charming of all these women, I mean why not, she was ex-girlfriend of Max, and had to be special. It had got very hard for Jay to convince Max for confronting her. Max was just not ready to, bring back all those good memories, I mean memories of past. He was scared on what if Anna manipulated him on getting Max back in her life. Seriously, now this was grand death of manhood. But Jay pumped him with weird ideas, and now they were going to meet up Anna in her fitness club. This evening as per schedule, she was there, while Jay and

Max were waiting outside the men section of club. They saw Anna, and Max went up to her. He gulped his hesitation and patted on her shoulders.

Max said, “Hey Anna, it’s nice to see you. How have you been doing?”.

Anna said, “Oh, of course it is. I mean I know its always nice to see me. I keep checking that in mirror.”.

Max smiled, “You haven’t changed even a bit. And look at us, we are so moved on.”.

Anna said, “Ha, that’s funny, because I was moving on, while you patted my back. So have we.”.

Jay interrupted, “She is right, I mean it was me who drove us here.”.

Max said, “Hey look, I am sorry, I really am, I am sorry for whatever happened between us. I am sorry for leaving you, I am sorry for not be able to give you what you deserved. I know you are little mad at me, because I have seen when and why this sarcasm comes out. But I want to tell you now, that I did this so we both could be happy in our lives. Anna we were not made for each other, and we both knew it the day we started living together. But now I think that maybe if I can go back in time, I could make things better than they were. But I am no Einstein and nor do I have a time machine, but I have a heart that wants to be friends with you.”.

Anna was flapping her towel for air on her face, “You know what Max, I am not mad at you. But I am mad at myself, on how can I make a mistake like you, on how did I even let you make the decision of leaving me, on how I allowed you to live with me to only know my imperfections. You are right, you can’t go back in time, nor can you go in future, but only if you knew how to live in the moment we spent together, things would have been different. And Max, I don’t want to be friends with you, in fact I pity on women who are in friendly terms with you. Ha.”.

Max said, “Your anger is justified, but you don’t have to shut your eyes whenever you see me.”.

Anna said, “I think its your eyes that are shut now. Don’t you see these shades I got from Dior.”.

Max said, "I heard you have a new boyfriend now, but what about friends.".

Anna snapped back, "You ignorant little boy, haven't you heard about women empowerment. Take this, I have been hitting this fitness club for last 3 months, and I am sure you don't want to know what I have learnt.".

Anna strode away while Jay said, "Max you sure she was your girlfriend, or the other way around.".

Anna, as fresh as breath could be, well these were the thoughts of Max who was clearly overwhelmed by confronting her. I mean all his fears had come true, with memories flashing in his eyes. He was clearly taken away. I mean it felt to Jay for a moment that it was Anna who was reading his mind, not Max. I mean seriously, but Anna was such a flashy woman, and she made it clear by mentioning Dior. One thing was sure that she still had emotions for Max, or such a pretentious woman would never talk to another man for that long. It could be that he was his ex, but then still an ex, and she had a new boyfriend. Just like Max, she could also have avoided a confrontation. She clearly said that Max didn't live in the moment. I mean that was little cliché, but true, as Max was always worried about future. But that was acceptable from a venture capitalist. But the point was that she clearly remembered what had happened between them, and she had held up grievances against him. With saying that the present could have been different, it clearly implied she would again not mind getting back with Max, though as a woman she would never show that. The point was that no matter Max had stopped her, she still had Max in her heart's corner, while refusing to move on him. She too was a qualified suspect, and had enough resources to pull this act off.

Now tailing and confronting these all suspects was over, and Jay was praying hardest that the mastermind be one of them, and she makes a mistake now. I mean all criminals were same. If you show you are weak in front of them, they would always pounce back on you. Saying sorry was not just to settle the differences, but also to provoke that particular woman. Both had reached back Max's home, where Jack was playing console games.

Max said, "Seriously, one of those women, hopefully, is making me do crimes, and it is me, Max, who goes up to them, and apologizes for something that wasn't even wrong, and you call yourself a detective.".

Jack interrupted, "Hey, Jay is also my friend, and you are insulting him. Many call him detective.".

Max exhaled, "And also I call you a friend. I mean, I am sorry Jack for thinking you as a friend.".

Jay calmed his shoulders, "Relax Max, you did a great job. I don't know if you were acting or this all came from heart, but expect something good coming your way.".

Jack said, "He is right, least you apologized. I mean that is what rare men do. Man like.".

Max said, "It has been days, that woman hasn't call. I hope meeting her, doesn't makes her ring back.".

Jay said, "Max, this woman is no more a woman, she is a criminal now, damn it she is blackmailing you, and all crimes are planned. If there is anything left that a man needs to do, you will get to know, or if what we have done today has worked, then you are the real man of the day, means no more man jobs.".

Night dawned, but seriously what would Max do of such a night, when 6 women from his past were haunting him like anything. This was just another sleepless night. Max could not forget face of Nova, when she would come by his house and threaten with help of his goony brother in laws to vacate the house. I mean she even justified that her family was too big to live in one house, so she wanted the house back. Back then Max always saw her as an enemy, but it was now he realized, how helpless even she was. He would not forget face of Ember, that had thrown Jose's undies on his face. I mean both Lucy and Jose were too young, but Max knew all Jose wanted was to have a score with pretty Lucy. Later Ember had requested Max that Lucy and Jose be sent to same college, when they were parting. Back then Max had thought of her as an imposing enemy who was trying to shape his brothers life, but it was now he had realized how hard it was to raise a sister all by herself.

Max couldn't forget face of Nina, who was pranked by Max into a little house party dressed as Juliet with Max's name tattooed on her hands. Back then, Max had thought her to be an obsessive freak girl, but it was now he realized how she must have felt to be made fun of from a crush. Max couldn't forget face of Molly standing beside the door while Max laughed in front of her father proposing marriage. Seriously for a minute back then Max had thought if they were joking, as everyone knew about his relationship with Stella, while Max and Molly hadn't seen each other for a while. It was then Max had saw a broken girl who would not let go of the door maybe in fear she would fall down and look weak. It was now Max had realized what it was to love somebody for all the time one could remember of.

Max woke up in a jolt and saw the clock to be at 3 AM. Damn it was still time. He held his head that was popping with memories. He took up his cellphone and texted to Jay, "Hey Jay. I don't know why, but the woman we are looking for is none of these 6. Let's meet after lunch, I will wrap things up early.".

Max fell again on his bed, trying to sleep, but this time it was Aspen. Max could not forget when he along with the companies fraud inspector, took Aspen from her office into custody. He clearly remembered her eyes that were always full of ideas, and spark, but the day they couldn't even look up. Back then Max had thought her to be just another prick trying to fool him. But it was now he realized that dreams neither are evil nor are good, they are just dreams. Max could never forget Anna's face when she had just returned shopping for a party to throw for Max on their anniversary, while Max waited for her with angst that every other day she found another excuse to empty their joint credit card limit. Back then, this was just an excuse to part away from a woman who was unrealistic. But it was now that Max realized, it was the way she was, and all her ways at some time had made him happy.

God, of all things that were happening, Max felt good that he least apologized to these women. Seriously, it wasn't manly, but it was so humanist. All these years Max had only lived with his version of what was right, and finally when a woman distorted his life, he was able to see what actually was right. Max couldn't sleep the entire night, but it was damn nice to be with these women in all those memories. It was morning, and been a while that Max had visited his office. So, the call was on, and he got himself dressing. He made himself breakfast, and got Alexaa speaking latest news. His phone rang, and there it was that Max no longer cared if it was that woman. He blindly picked it.

Daisy said, "Hey Max my boy. I am sorry for shouting at you the other day. But you deserved that. Anyways listen, I and Fred are going out today to attend an evening party. Don't ask me whose it is. So you have to pick Esther from her school and just bring back home. Fred's mother has an injury, so she can't drive, but will keep her company.".

Max said, "Come on Daisy, since when did you started apologizing to a driver.".

Daisy snapped back, "Not just a driver, but one that is driving our family crazy. Anyways what about that woman.".

Max clichéd, "Forget it, already one woman named Molly has drifted us apart.".

Daisy said, "Okay. And wait, Fred wanted to talk with you about something. So call him, Okay, Bye.".

Max exhaled while he held the glass of milk in his other hand. Of course Max liked milk, especially this flavored one, but picking up Esther was like getting back into stone age and act like a donkey. But that was okay, she was sweet, and would definitely grow up into one hell of a woman, wait, not that kind of woman, but a good kind of woman. Max got driving, and was somehow feeling good. It felt like this was all over, as Jay had said, apologies end greatest of crisis. Max turned his favorite podcast on, and in no time he was again back at HQ of Catalyzers. The guard smiled to see him back, while the floor waved their hands at Max, while he strode into his office to find Jeff sitting with bunch of young men, apparently startup founders. Seriously, this was what Max liked the most, talking about possibilities, changing the world, setting new standards, bringing ground breaking methods on table, and working on latest technologies. Max got on his chair, while he shook hands with Jeff. Few minutes passed.

Max said, “I think you people don’t want funds. Because clearly you are wasting time that is money.”.

One founder started speaking, “Oh to the point Max. We are trying to change how working class will have their meals in future. The sector is highly unorganized and unhealthy. This is where we come in, with customized menus, flexible schedule, pay per meal option, and accessibility in every corner of this city.”.

Max clichéd, “Come on, tell me something that makes my hand reach for the cheque book.”.

The startup founder smiled confidently, “Okay. I want to see your signatures.”.

Max looked at Jeff, “Are you sure, because I also sign on Rejection letters. Anyways thanks for the pitch.”.

The young founders went out of his office, while Jeff high fived him. “Hey guess who’s back in the business. Hey Max, seriously man I missed you. By the way, you have 20 more pitches to follow up with. So take your time, to think about creative ideas on how to reject them, as board has already met its quota for this quarter.”.

Max said, “You know someday I am going to reject this job that doesn’t makes me feel like an investor.”.

Jeff laughed and got to this cubicle, while Max did gave time to read through all those 20 proposals. I mean seriously, what was even the point of reading these proposals if none have to be approved. But then this was how the goodwill of Catalyzers have shadowed the market, to be one of the most empathetic investors, the reason why all the young founders of the city first came to them. But anyways rejecting them was also an art, I mean Max in all of his career had never said a direct no to any founder. This was his reputation. Then his phone rang.

The woman said, “Hey Max, how does it feels to be a man. I am sure you missed me, because I so did.”.

Max exhaled, “How can I miss you when you just keep calling again and again.”.

The woman said, “Ha, ha. Anyways tell me. What is it that man lives for? What is it that man leaves behind?”.

Max snapped back, “Oh I will be able to tell that, only if you could let me live.”.

The woman said, “The answer is simple, his legacy. Now that I want you to be a man, so you have to create a legacy for yourself. You know I have always loved Robinhood for his manhood, so we will do this his way. You have to rob a rich man who keeps his entire wealth in his home, and distribute that wealth amongst poor. Trust me all rich men are dirty, and you will be doing good.”.

Max snapped back, “Wow, all this time I only thought that you wanted to ruin just my life.”.

The woman said, “Ha ha, Max you are also funny at times. But listen carefully, if you do not do so, you will loose all your hard earned money resting now in your bank accounts. For starters, I have already emptied your National Bank account. Don’t panic it were just 50k dollars, but you should, when I will empty the rest of them.”.

The woman continued, “By the way, it was nice meeting you after a long time.”.

Max crushed his phone to hit back on table. Shit, Jay was right, it was one of those 6 women. God, they were no saints. Damn it, there she did, telling something about her. But wait, his National Bank account was emptied. Hell no. Max quickly opened his account on his laptop, to only see that all his money was withdrawn into an offshore account. God, now this woman also knew hacking. By the way, Max had saved money in his National Bank account for his children’s education. Guess they were all going to learn about Robinhood. God no, was this woman crazy, now Max had to rob a man. I mean which man becomes a man after robbing another man. Max was still being watched, and he looked up to see the CCTV cameras, god no, this woman had her hands deep down in Max’s life.

Seriously who could be it, Nina, Ember, Anna, or Molly, or Nova, or Aspen. God no, this wasn’t over, and this shouldn’t have been happening again. Just when Max had thought this to be over, it felt things had just got started. Breaking a leg was okay, fucking a woman was also bearable, but now he had to commit a serious crime. Max called Jay and Jack to reach his home immediately, while he left in hurry, as he had a fortune to save. I mean no way, Max was loosing his hard earned money to a crazy woman. The shit had just got real, I mean now it was about Max's own existence. Seriously loose all your money or rob someone's entire wealth, I mean the choices were so great.

Chapter 15

Jay said, "Now we know, it is one of them, and she wants you to rob another man.".

Jack said, "Thank god that this one of them isn't fan of Jack the ripper. Just saying.".

Max snapped back, "This woman is crazy. She won't stop until we catch her. You know she has no emotions for me. God now she is going to make me bankrupt if I don't rob a man. And I know she will do it, because this woman is scared of nothing, at least not us. This woman has no limits.".

Jack said, "Hey not us, but you both. You haven't introduced me to these ladies.".

Jay said, "Her Philosophy is simple, either win or lose, while stakes remain the same.".

Jack interrupted, "Seriously, now you are doing a thesis on this woman, I thought we needed to catch her.".

Max said, "Hey I cannot rob a man of his entire wealth. I mean this is just not me. I know how much money matters, as all my life I have helped people with money and made it the hard way. Plus it is a crime. Soon the local police will be on it, and I am sure that a private detective and an idiot friend cannot save me from the consequences. I cannot let this woman, turn me into henchman if not a man.".

Jack said, "I agree, that Jeff is such an idiot. But you forgot me, can't I watch your back.".

Jay continued, "Wait, you are scared of Police right, and you are not getting the right feeling of robbing somebody. I have an idea, and trust me no police will get involved, only if you rob another rich criminal. Simple rob a robber, and robber will never go to the police, and you will never have a guilt of robbing somebody. And Max, I am not just a detective, but a friend of a friend, which makes us also friends, and we are in it together. Also don't get me wrong. But you have to pay me, and you have also to pay your bills. So save those bank accounts, while we catch her.".

The final words of Jay had put some sense in Max. His hesitation was gone for a bit and for a while. Max agreed, while Jay assured that he knew many criminals that they could rob, of course Max would choose which one of them, while Jay would suggest who will be the easiest one to. For a minute Max thought all of this to be unreal, but then he thanked god that had given him friends by his side in these tough times. Seriously, any man that would grow up to become an venture capitalist would dream last of robbing somebody in his entire life, and our Max was no exception. So here it was destiny calling Max to be a Robinhood of 21st century. But seriously, he wouldn't be leaving his day job to keep robbing rich people, it was just for once, it was just so Max could save his own back. Max consoled himself that what he was doing to do was a good crime, I mean robbing a robber was no sin, and god would definitely forgive him for that. Plus doing this crime was his only way of stopping another crime that would ruin his life.

For a minute it felt it was Nova, with all that ancestral grudge, after all Robinhood anecdote was also historical. Jay would not have been a very good detective, as he had clearly failed in catching that woman, but his past was sure going to come in handy. I mean all the criminals he had known. Max had done window shopping a lot in his past, but today he was out to do window criminal shopping. Yes, Jay and Max had both got riding in his car to see few criminals, and decide which one to rob. Jay was driving around, while Max was feeling uneasy like any other man, yes any other normal man. They made their first stop at house of Bobby, he was a thug.

Jay said, "You see there man in shorts. He is Bobby, a scammer, a fraud, and a thug. Now Max, all these people I am going to show you, keep their booties in their houses. You know they can't deposit heir black money in banks. This one Bobby also owns street muscle, as you can see those other men around him, they are always there.".

Max said, "You know those shorts are okay, but not that gun tucked in them.".

Jay said, “Hey Max Listen, I too have one of those, and if necessary will use it. I am not leaving you.”.

Max said, “Its good to hear, but if I don’t do it alone, that woman too isn’t leaving me.”.

Jay said, “I know that, now listen the most important thing. He keeps all his money in a big safe on the first floor of his house. It is where his family lives too, his wife and his 2 daughters. He has a perfect housewife who always stays in kitchen, while his daughters are always synched into punk rock. Plus he never lets his men get near his family. So the floor can be all yours, once you sneak in. The best way in is through roof, and it’s the best way out too.”.

Max exhaled, “That’s okay, let’s see more of them. I mean least you can give me more choices.”.

Back when Jay was a police officer, he had once raided Bobby’s house, and this was only couple of years ago. Bobby had cheated Jewel trader by giving him fake diamonds in return of gold. That Jewel trader had filed report against Bobby, and it was when Jay had raided his house and found his safe. During his times Jay was a much feared police man, and Bobby too had got scared of the consequences. So Bobby made a pact with Jay that he will return all of the gold to that trader, and Jay just settled this crime and overlook what all other stuff he got in the safe. Jay had been a good man, and believer of school of thought that criminals are made not born. He agreed, but it was then Jay had realized that this Bobby kept all of his wealth in that safe.

For now Jay was betting hard that he hadn’t moved his safe since then, in fact while driving he had also confirmed that with one of his sources. Robbing Bobby might not have been easy, but it was easiest to have all the time required to crack the safe. Max was already thinking on his spider man skills on how he would manage to topple over roofs to land on Bobby’s. I mean he has always enjoyed it on Television, but it was now he was developing a deep respect for those who really did it. All those childhood desires of being a vigilante and social hero were becoming true for Max. Would Max become great by doing this, I mean it didn’t looked like if he was going to get some gallantry award for this. Max just prayed that this ended soon. Now they had driven into the Chumswick district, the most infamous and notorious neighborhood of Nightindale. Jay stopped the car in front of a house, a house that belonged to Billy.

Jay said, "You see that statue in front of that house, it's of Billy. Ah, he is no dead, but the people around believe him to be greater than god, so they got that statue made. In his crime career up till 2 years back, he had robbed 7 banks, and always walked free. If my intel is right he has a wardrobe as good as stuffed with money as of a small community bank. I know you aren't interested in his money, as anyways it will go to poor. But just saying.".

Max said, "I wish he remained a statue while I rob his booty.".

Jay said, "I know his confidence levels, the last thing he would expect is someone robbing his place.".

Max said, "Yeah, and it will be the last thing I will be doing, if caught.".

Jay said, "Hey it's just a robbery, in our country a robbery takes place every 5 seconds. Now listen the most important thing. This wardrobe that has his entire wealth, is kept in his room on ground floor. He has 5 brothers, but is on bitter terms with them, so actually they would not mind if a small screams comes out of his room. The best news, is that Billy is a 65 Year old man, who has diabetes and over sleeps. Now the bad news is that these 6 brothers have 9 sons that too live in the house. They are the ones you need to take care of.".

Max exhaled, "You know how a robbery takes place every 5 seconds, because police gets to know it.".

Jay shrugged, as paranoia of being caught had completely taken over Max. But then Max too realized that Billy was sort of an easy target. I mean he had to break into a room where a man would probably be asleep, and the money will be in a wardrobe, while the robbery will happen as quick as changing clothes. But those 9 son of guns were the problem. Back when Jay was a police officer, he was made to work on a bank robbery that happened in Chumswick district. The prime suspect of the robbery was Billy and obviously his home was raided and it was then Jay found about this wardrobe, and even then in this wardrobe were found thousands of dollars. But Billy was smart, and he proved in court that this money was earned by his farming. Well Billy had no huge farm lands, or else why he would be robbing banks, but he had small farm in his house backyard. By showing fake invoices he proved that lemons that grew in his backyard were sold to foreign companies and it was where he earned that money. On being asked, how can a lemon be sold in thousands of dollars, Billy said that he had a rare species of lemons back from thousand of years. The case went on and Billy walked free.

On this day too Billy had the same wardrobe he used for his medical expenses and needs, as per a source. Robbing Billy was really simple, only if Max didn't encountered his sons sitting in lobby and betting on baseball matches. Max was already thinking of ways on how to enter his house and get away with all the dirt money. Seriously this was the point of life where he had to think such things too. For now Jay had driven them in front of another house which was owned by Marlow.

Jay said, "See those cars parked outside that house. Well they all are stolen. Over there on porch, is Marlow. He is a street crime lord, and all the neighborhoods give him a cut of their earnings. He is sort of maintenance, or trouble shooting criminal. Whenever there is a dispute between thugs, his words are final. He can be our man, because he too keeps his entire wealth in his house, in a safe just across the living room.".

Max exhaled, "Seriously is there any life beyond that living room, or dead end, like dead.".

Jay said, "I know him, he trusts every one coming to his house. It'll help you.".

Max said, "But you know what, I don't trust him. I don't trust criminals.".

Jay said, "Of course you don't, and you should never. Now listen carefully, all his wealth is in that safe just across the hall you can see. The good news is, that every evening, thugs from all around the neighborhood visit his house, and just walk up to that safe to put their cut, and while so, there is nobody in the safe room. Trust me Max, walking up an open safe has never been easier. All you have to figure is on how to get all the booty out from his house. This is the easiest crime scene you will ever get. You have three choices, now make a call.".

Max thought for a while, "I think the robber of robbers, the Robinhood too wants his cut.".

There it was, Max had finalized that they were going to Rob Marlow. But still the problem was same, on how they would get that money out from the house. They waited and kept a close eye on all movements in and out of the house. By the way, back then when Jay was a police officer, he was handed to crack down the street robberies in city. He knew it that ending such a huge network can only happen when he would cut off their network hubs. To do so, Jay took an initiative of freezing all funds of their leaders, and Marlow was one of them. It was when Jay saw his safe, and yes he froze it too. During the raid, Jay had noticed that thugs simply walked in to keep their cut of stash. To confirm if it was still in practice, Jay had checked it with his sources. I mean every other thug who obviously were also bastards, knew about this walk into me safe, but till this date no one had dared robbing it.

But anyways, there is always the first time, and the ribbon was going to be cut by Max. Walking into Marlow's safe was simple. Walk into his house, tell his servant from which neighborhood you have came from, and tell him the amount you were here to give, and walk inside the safe, keep it there, and walk out. Though Max had just not to walk out, but empty the safe and then walk out. One simple way was creating a ruckus, and coming out on gunpoint. But Jay wasn't sure if Max would be able to do it. So they vigilantly kept their eyes, to find one weak link. The day was ending, while Max and Jay returned back home. Max was exhausted, while they had discussed a final plan for the heist, and prayed that it worked. Max walked in to find Daisy sitting on his couch.

Daisy said, "Oh its nice to see, you still remember your house, because you've clearly forgotten your family.".

Fred said, “I know you dislike me, now is it same with my daughter.”.

Max held his head, “Hey Daisy, I am really sorry. And Fred, for me she is my niece, and never you daughter.”.

Fred said, “Daisy asked you one simple thing, and you forgot, while you complain that Daisy never calls you. You know what, now she won’t. Max, it’s simple to say a No. Like, No, I can’t do it.”.

Max said, “Fred, I would never give a second thought of saying a no to you, because I do treat you a family. And Daisy I am sorry, I was stuck, and it was damn important, I can’t tell you now.”.

Daisy said, “You know Esther waited for you the entire day, entire evening. She didn’t ate anything, she was scared. What could be more important to you than your own family.”.

Fred said, “Come on Daisy, he was stuck. He must have got lucky with some other Maya.”.

Daisy said, “Max you are losing it. You are losing your own family. But still I have faith in my brother. The brother I used to know. So finish all your important stuff, while your family still waits. Or else it will be too late. In fact it is quite late, and we should be going. Good Bye Max.”.

Daisy and Fred got walking out, while Max kicked on his couch. Damn, how could he miss picking up Esther. I mean it would have barely taken an hour, but no he was busy watching the dirtiest of criminals in the city. Just because of one woman, Stella now hated Max, and now Daisy too was drifting apart. This woman was taking every thing that Max loved away from him. Despite of fact that Max was listening to this woman because of his friends and family, no one would understand what Max was feeling, cheated, deceived and abandoned. I mean what was the use of picking Esther, if Max had no money to refuel his car, or take Esther to her favorite ice cream parlor.

Max said, “Jay now as you can see what this woman is doing. I want this to end.”.

Jay said, “Take it easy Max, your family can only see what you are doing.”.

Max made Jay stay over his house, till they pulled off this heist. For the first time in all these days, Max was feeling lonely, and so targeted. He was feeling vulnerable, after his family had hit hard where it hurt. Maybe this woman also knew that Daisy had told Max to pick Esther earlier this morning, and she intentionally called Max the same day to break this Robinhood saga. God, this woman didn't wanted to make Max a man, but a man who would lose everything including his peace, his family, his senses, and his true self. I mean she had now admitted that they have met, so it had to be one of those 6 women. It was nice meeting after a long, made sense only for Anna, because she was the only one that Max met often, in fact they stayed together.

The night went on, while Max changed sides on his bed, only to look at Jay sleeping sound on the couch. God, was Max the only man who had lost his sleep in all of this scene. He turned his WhatsApp on to only see that Stella too was online. Of course, he was not alone, another life too was broken. The entire night Max kept watching Display picture of Stella and soon it was morning. Max and Jay waited further till it was evening. They were back now on his car, to park outside Marlow's house. The plan was in place, and Max was holding on to his nerves. Max couldn't have made a mistake, because he knew that Jay's confidence on this situation was vague especially considering Marlow's punters around, who could easily take out both Jay and Max, to dispose their bodies, and no one would ever know what actually happened. For this day, Jay had even got a pistol for Max, in case if things went out of his hands.

But seriously, only Max knew that this too was vague, as Max would never ever shoot anybody. He was not a killer, nor a criminal. Jay's eyes were fixed on watch, and the other eye on people entering Marlow's house with their gang's cut. The time had came, Max stepped out and went inside with confidence he usually had with Unicorn startup founders. He stopped to wave hands at Marlow who was busy chatting with someone on phone. He turned around to his servant.

Max said, "From Chumswick, I have got 3 thousand dollars, business is weak.".

The servant nodded, “I hope that it’s the business, not the intentions that are weak.”.

Max kept walking, while servant hesitated for a minute, “Hey, wait. I already have an entry for Chumswick, by Javier. Then who the hell are you.”.

Two more men sitting in the hall, got alerted, while they slowly reached for their guns. Marlow who was speaking on phone, appeared had his other ear on them, as he too hanged the phone to look at Max. The situation in the hall had got stiffened. The plan apparently had a loophole, while Max felt the sweat on his face.

Max said, “I was sent by Billy’s son. Do you want me to tell him, who the hell is he.”.

Marlow started laughing, “Ha, ha. Let him go. What the hell are you even doing? He brings money.”.

Chapter 16

Max kept walking inside, till he reached the safe. There it was, a huge iron safe that was open. I mean what in the world could be better than standing in front of an open safe. Yeah, especially ask this to a man who wants to rob the same safe. There it was all the money, in fact for a minute Max thought that it was better to be a thug than a venture capitalist. I mean in all of his years working hard he had never been able to earn that much of money which was resting in one shelf of the safe. Seriously, why did Max had to be Robinhood. I mean he could have taken all this money and said no to that woman. Go ahead, take my money, I have more than what you will take, was what Max wanted to say. But wait, Max wasn't a robber.

He waited there for a minute and turned around to talk to another man sitting outside the safe room. Servant got little suspicious, and watched Max while he talked. Then servant got busy with his entries of money. Max waited for a while, went inside another couple of rooms escaping all eyes, and strode out. He walked out like a king, while Marlow smiled at him. He strode out, and directly went back into his car where Jay waited. Max had done what he was there to do.

Jay said, "Tell me it is done, and no one saw you. Of course no one saw you.".

Max said, "Yeah it is done. And everyone saw me, but wait, not doing that. Ha.".

Jay said, "I know this feeling Max. I have served 5 years of my life chasing it. But it still is good.".

Max and Jay waited, and waited. Their heist was not done. Few other people came in and went out, while they both kept waiting. The watch had struck its time, and there it was. Max and Jay walked out of their car, again up till Marlow's house. They looked around and came back with all the money.

Jay said, "That is hell lot of money. Are you sure you want to be Robinhood.".

Max said, "Like if anybody cares what I want to be. Now Jay the legacy is made, find that woman, please.".

Jay and Max went up to the slummiest of area in Nightindale to distribute the money. And seriously, the people they gave this money too, were one sight that happened in a lifetime. They couldn't believe it. Some said, 'He is back', while the other said, 'He is Godsend', while someone also said, 'We are not giving this back to you.'. Overall, few homeless guys were about to check in to Hilton, Marriott, and maybe Disney Resorts. While Max did it, it quite felt to be great, In fact Max had never did any thing even close like this. Was this legacy in building, Max didn't knew it, but sure these people would never forget Max's face, and maybe tell their children about this. Wait, now how did this money came.

Let's go back a bit, while Max went inside he had a super light fabric bag hiding in his chest. So he took all the money from the safe to stuff inside the bag. He came out and talked the other man to distract everybody. Then again he sneaked inside to take the bag to the kitchen, while the cook of house like everyday was serving evening coffee to Marlow at 6:30. Max quickly emptied all the money into the trash bag in kitchen. His work was done, he came out with bare hands. They waited till 7 PM, when the cook's shift ended, and he took the kitchen trash bag along with him to dump outside, while he said goodbye to servant and Marlow. So now the money was out, and Jay and Max were on it. Seriously, robbing someone was not that difficult. Now Marlow would never know who actually robbed him, and could never go to the police to file report of missing black money. Jay and Max were the winner, and they were now hitting a local bar where Jack insisted that they celebrated this cause. Max was not in mood, but Jay took him anyway. They sat and were few drinks down.

Jack laughed, "You people actually made one of the people of one of the nastiest criminals, bring all that money out from their house. I mean we should do this often, and will soon retire in Malibu.".

Jay smiled, "Malibu has both a prison and a graveyard. So be specific.".

Jack burped, "Seriously guys, this is a skill. Like I have of throwing parties that are paid off by guests.".

Jay said, "That is not a skill, but poverty. Hey wait, I am sorry, but we have already given away all the booty to your brothers. So I think you should consider a family reunion rather than celebrating with us.".

Jack said, "You know I can buy my drinks, but sadly I don't have change for your crap.".

Jay and Jack argued, while Max sipped on to his drink. Max looked around the club, and could see few rugged men, likes of ones that had beaten him, then there was a biker on other corner pouring a jar of beer down, then few odd women who clearly were in the club solely to get laid, and lastly few bunch of thugs who were the in the club to celebrate maybe their recent crime. It was all there, with Max who for a minute felt like a man who had conquered all such people. Then Max's phone rang, and a silence followed. Jay, Jack and Max were looking at each other.

The woman said, "Well done Max, my man. But seriously, I don't know what are you celebrating for. I wanted you to be Robinhood, not some guilt fighting bloke. I told you to rob a rich man, and what you did was listen to your conscious and that Jay. Max, robbing Marlow doesn't makes you ideally a Robinhood. So guess what.".

Max snapped back, "I also listened to you, and did exactly like you said.".

The woman said, "No you didn't, now listen me again very carefully, rob a rich man, not a thug, who keeps their entire wealth in home, and the robbed money should be least 1 million, yes that is the penalty of doing this wrong, along with a penalty of 25 thousand dollars that have been emptied from your central bank account. Rest remains same, distribute it amongst poor. I hope you do this right this time.".

Max said, "Of course a man with 1 million will be rich. Thanks for the mention.".

Woman had hanged the phone, Jay said, "How could she make you do this again.".

Max waved his head, "Just like she vanished 25 thousand dollars from account again. God. Jay, you know what, this will keep happening, unless you show me how good a detective you are.".

Jay said, "I think its Nina. You know, she is the only woman with access to public eyes. Or second best its Molly, who is still friends with Daisy and knows everything about you.".

Jack said softly, "Hey, but don't we need to rob a rich man first. Because I don't want this party to be the last party that Max throws. I can't see you like that Max.".

Max said, "Oh nice to know that you can see me robbing, least. Now who keeps 1 million in their home.".

Jack slowly interrupted, "Mr. and Mrs. Chester from Blooms Arcade. The last time I checked.".

Max and Jay both looked back at Jack, who didn't had the best feeling in the world while he said that. But he was sure that Mr. and Mrs. Chester had close to 1 million dollars in their house safe, and it was the all money that they had. I mean these people didn't trusted banks. They were no criminal, and still had such huge stash in their house. But how did Jack knew it. Of course, he did, because Chester family was his client. Yes Jack was a public accountant, and like many other clients, Chester family too sought suggestions on taxes, investments, and other financial moves from Jack. In fact only a week ago Jack had visited Chester family and their safe. As per Jack, they were the easiest catch Max could ever have. By the way Mr. Chester was an 65 year old man, while Mrs. Chester was an 63 year old woman. They also had children, but they were all settled in Kingdom of Isles. They visited their parents only once in a while. So this couple lived alone with their servants in their huge mansion. Their old age was also the reason they kept all their money in their house.

For now this much detail was enough for Jay, and Max, while all three of them returned to Max's house, to make a plan on how to rob Chester couple. Finally there it was, a true robbery, a true robbery of rich couple, exactly like Robinhood would have done it. The night went on, while Jack explained every single detail about their safe, their habits, and their routine. Jack knew them very closely. In fact Chester family would trust Jack with their safe, that was the level of trust.

Max said, "How do I rob an old couple, they are my parents age. I mean its wrong.".

Jay said, "That woman is also your sister's age Max. Do you think it's right to hate her.".

Max said, "Robbing Marlow was different. It was black money, and apparently police won't care who robbed Marlow. But now we are talking about respectable citizens of society, The Chester Family. The consequences could finish me, Jay. There is no right feeling about this.".

Jay said, "Max I don't know about that woman, but right now I want you to be man. Trust me nothing worse will happen, their son will come to take these oldies back to kingdom of Isles. But if you don't do this, your car outside will be towed away, and your engagement ring will go on to some pawn shop.".

Max interrupted, "Hey, this car is not going away, but 1 million for sure are coming out.".

All three went on to sleep. Someone on couch, someone on carpet, and wait was there someone on dining table too. Clearly Stella was not in home. After a long, Max had slept a sound sleep. But was it booze that helped this night, or the warmth of 2 good friends. But seriously, Max had started to get in doubt, if Jay was even a police officer in past. I mean what kind of police officer he would have been. Since the day he had joined Max, all he has done was give crazy ideas on how to fulfill whims of that woman. His job was to catch that woman, last Max could remember, but apparently what he did was scare Max on what would happen if he didn't broke a leg, or didn't rob a rich man. Seriously, one thing was sure that Jay indeed was Jack's friends. Of course Jay had became close to Max as well, but his roots belonged with Jack. Seriously, Jay was too influenced by criminals, which was obvious when every time he got excited in doing one. I mean he knew how criminals thought, and how they did it.

So was he right, could it be Nina, or could it be Molly. Well his theory behind wasn't too bad. But first this heist needed to be pulled out, and then these ladies be taken care of delicately, because clearly they could have harmed Max. Morning has came, and Jack was making breakfast while Jay and Max interestingly watched the news. The reporter said, 'Messiah of Nightindale makes a comeback.', while other said, 'These Homeless people are not alone in this.', and a sub reporter was saying, 'Where did this money came from. Who has that kind of money to give in charity.'. While on some other channel the news said, 'It is the communists. People, see this man, covered in crap, he could be your next neighbor. He claims he has that kind of money'. While the man screamed, 'It takes a man to help another man.'. Max smiled at Jay, while the first phase of plan was to start. Max picked the phone, while both okayed.

Max said, "Hello Mr. Chester, how have you been doing. I've heard that doctor has increased the dose for your heart ache. I understand it must be hard. So I will break this slowly. I am going to rob your safe very soon, and that 1 million of booty will be mine. Guess what, you can do nothing about it, so don't worry, and absolutely do not give your heart a ride. And convey my regards to Mrs. Chester.".

Mr. Chester said, "It's been long I haven't used my guns. Try that, and I will warm them up.".

Max hanged the phone, while Mr. Chester kept speaking. Jay said, "I think he bought it.".

Jack interrupted, "Of course he did. He is an avid collector of hand guns. Huge fan.".

Max shrugged, "Hey Jack, you go and keep an eye, and not on his collections but movement.".

Jay and Max got riding and their stop was the factory where Mr. Chester's safe was made. Yeah, it was a local factory and made unique safes for all their customers. This was the Phase 2 of plan. Jay and Max waited outside the factory, for their phone to ring. No they weren't waiting for that woman to call, but Jack. Max was getting impatient, on what was taking so long, had the plan failed. No it can't, because this was the best shot they had got. Did Mr. Chester called the police, of course not or by now Jack must have called them to let know. As per Jack, the last thing

Mr. Chester would do was calling the police and disclosing the huge amount they kept in their house. Finally the call came in, and Jack okayed that the plan was working. Max and Jay went inside, and first thing was that they met the Salesman. Well Jay and Max were here to act like they were going to buy a safe.

Max said, “Hey we want to buy your Z300 model safe. Heard many good things about it.”.

The salesman said, “Of course you have, because bad things don’t happen with our safes.”.

Jay said, “Yeah, on point. Hey I was curious, if there is any way to break your safes.”.

The salesman shrugged, “I am glad that you asked it. So let me tell that in our past history of 75 years, we have never ever repaired any safe. I mean they are completely unbreakable, by all means. You know what sir, once you buy this thing, your generations will have to bear with this. And seriously, the only thing it has got broken is records of seamless safety for years. But still, we strongly recommend that you keep your safes maintained with latest additions, and features.”.

Max said, “Okay, I am convinced, but a little scared if I will be able to access my money if forget the keys.”.

They laughed, but the salesman didn’t knew that their record was about to be broken. Jay and Max had got what they have wanted, a full demo of the same safe that was installed in Mr. Chester’s house. Now they knew everything about it, and particularly that thing which they wanted to know. Meanwhile, Jack was still keeping an eye on Mr. Chester’s house, tracking all his movements. Everything was working as they have planned. Jack knew that Mr. Chester was a very precautious man, and he did exactly as they had wanted, after that warning. Soon it was evening, while Jay and Max had joined Jack just outside Mr. Chester’s house. They waited, and waited. Soon, the house servant’s shift was over, as he walked out.

Now this huge mansion had only two people living inside, Mr. Chester, and Mrs. Chester. You know what was tricky about branded things, that they all had pattern. So Mr. Chester’s house door was no exception, it was made by city’s best furniture maker, which also came with a lock made by same furniture maker. Now, one man can't be good at two things, so this house lock had a loop, that Jay somehow had figured with his old thief sources, but the trickiest part was that unbreakable safe. They waited more, till Mr. and Mrs. Chester had their dinner and went up to their bedroom. There it was, the lights went on, as they could see through the window. The time was closing in, and soon these lights would also go off.

Max said, "You know I have never visited a house without an invitation, and now I am breaking in. God.".

Jay said, "Have your bank accounts been emptied before by a crazy woman criminal.".

Jack said, "Yeah, and what about crashing in my apartment. It might not be a house, but its still a place.".

Max said, "Okay, Okay. I got it. By the way Jack, every time I had visited your apartment uninvited was to drop you off when you were too drunk to even stand. But its okay, now I will not. And Jay, not before now, I had never hired a detective, and neither will I in future, because I think friends are just enough. So thanks both of you.".

Jay and Jack looked at each other, thinking Max was acting little crazy, but why would he not, even these both were getting the chills of this legit robbery. Anyways, everything was going as they had wished, unless Mr. Chester had an appetite for acting and was planning a surprise for this phone call burglar. Max hadn't said it nor had he asked, but he was curious on where this collection of handguns was, hopefully not in his bedroom where he was about to sleep now. Of course not, people kept such collections in their living room or study room, which in this case was one floor down. So this had kept Max cool for a while. But seriously, it had been close to 10, why was Mr. Chester still awake. What if their plan and making the morning call had back fired. Wait, the lights went off, and so did Jay and Jack showed a thumbs up sign.

Max quickly wore a mask, and was headed slowly to the house's door. Seriously, robbing a house was so not Max's thing. And wait, that woman wanted Max to leave a legacy behind, I mean would Max want his children to talk about the creepiness of this act. Thankfully there were no dogs in the house. In no time Max unlocked the front door, and in next minute he was there in the room with safe in front of his eyes. There it was a lock with 1 million behind that were anyways never going to be of Max, as he was Robinhood of 21st century. God, Max thought, one mistake and he would rot in jail or die of septic after being shot by a vintage handgun. This was the moment, when fear crept in. Then a huge alarm went off, to even wake the neighbors. Hoot, Hoot!

Chapter 17

Mr. Chester rose from bed, “He is here, and he is robbing us. I am going to kill him.”.

Mrs. Chester in panic followed him, “A robbery is enough, no more crimes for the night.”.

Chester couple, got running towards the other end of house but on first floor. While striding out Mr. Chester had picked one of his handgun. Well, this collection of handgun was there is almost every room of the house, hung as an art piece. Apparently, Jack had only seen the living room hall and the safe room. Chester couple hurried to get hold of Max, while he did the robbery. By the way, earlier this day, when the Max had called Mr. Chester to tell him that Max would rob the safe. Mr. Chester had got upgraded the alarm system of safe, with higher pitch siren, with a distress message to be delivered to nearest Patrol Police car. If somebody entered the wrong key, this alarm would go off. By the way, at any given point of time, a Patrol Police car was only 2 minutes from any house in Blooms Town. Mr. Chester knew that Max would not be able to run too far. He entered the room and saw somebody, well Max, jumping out from window, while scattering money stuffed in a bag.

Mr. Chester in anger hit his handgun on wall, “God I knew this would happen. I had sensed it. Hey, you go, and wait at the door, a policeman must be on his way. This thief cannot run too far.”.

Mrs. Chester got moving, “He doesn’t needs to get too far, but only far out of sight. Just saying.”.

Mr. Chester yelled, “Why does it sounds like, if this was only my money. Go.”.

Mrs. Chester went down striding, and instead of waiting she had opened the door, with another handgun in her hands. Guess it ran in the family. While upstairs, Mr. Chester was now thinking that the bag Max carried was not that big to carry all money out. He opened the safe to see how much was he robbed. What, he felt astounded, to see all the money was in place. Mr. Chester slowly turned around to only find Max spraying anesthesia on his face. Mr. Chester soon got unconscious, but while falling down his hands took the mask down from Max's face, for Mr. Chester to see a blurred face of Max. Max quickly went up to the safe, and collected all money. Every single bit of it. He had stolen it all.

The big 1 million heist was done, and Max again jumped out from the window, while Mrs. Chester kept waiting for a police man to appear. Mr. Chester was a fallen man, and he was not going to wake up back at least for next 4 to 5 hours. Max ran back to the car, where Jay and Jack were impatiently waiting for the hero of the day, or maybe the villain of Chester Family, or least a Robinhood of 21st century. Max got in, and smiled back as he showed the bag. Hell lot of money it was, but charity money. They drove out.

Max said, "God, it worked like a charm. You know step by step, exactly like we planned.".

Jack said, "First time in my career I am unlikely happy to see my client go bankrupt.".

Jay said, "While this is the third time that an award winning ex-policeman is helping a crime get done.".

Max said, "Hey, in fact, even I am the first venture capitalist in history of finance that is going to give away 1 million dollars for free, for nothing, for charity.".

Jack took out a bottle of water and said, "Cheers to Wall Street Robinhood, and cheers to that woman.".

Seriously, this was the most manly thing Max had ever done in life. I mean considering that most of the thieves, robbers and criminals were men. Plus, somehow this woman had made Max closer to his friends. Though the heist was over, but Max was still little scared, if he did something wrong this time too and that woman was on her way to call him and rob maybe 10 more millions. But time passed, and no call showed up. By the way what had happened was that Max and Jay had got the tune of that alarm from safe factory, and Max had played the tune simply to indicate that someone was trying to rob Mr. Chester. He bought it, with that cash falling from bag, and himself opened the safe for Max. Ha, ha, ha. All three of them had now driven to the Night

Square, the center of city with fountain at mid of the circle, which always had poor homeless people sleeping around it. Max saw them, and it felt like if Max was there hero. I mean this money could get these people shelter for days, food for month, and hope for a lifetime. I mean did really the society needed a Robinhood.

But wait, robbing rich men, especially ones with good taste in handguns was too risky. Jay while in car, blew the horn to rise them all. And one by one, Max handed them fistful of bundles of money. A man from other corner shouted, 'he is the same man, he gives money to poor'. This was the moment, and this was a legacy, though short, but a fine one. While Max handed them money, they won't let go of his hands, as if saying with eyes, do not go. Max smiled amidst all adversities, amidst the fact that he was a criminal, his fiancé was gone, his sister was drifting apart, there were 6 women that hated him, but this smile, no one could have taken away. He felt like, doing good things was easy, more easier than he had thought, and maybe he should do it in a bit by bit, though of course not by robbing people. While Max left, he received salutes, hats down, and flying kisses by few young fellows. I mean it did felt manly, and for a minute it felt like living for this was worth enough. All three were back in Max's home, the night went by, and the morning had started with news.

Anchor said, "I knew it was communists. I mean who other than a drunk Russian can have 1 million dollars to spare. This is a ploy against our city, to spoil the poor with money, free money.".

Another guest debated him, "Oh can poor be even spoiled by money. You can do better than that.".

An angry politician said, "This free money, if given again and again, these poor will turn criminals. Because I know there is no addiction worse than money.".

A man replied, "I think there is no addiction worse than staying hungry. This man is a hero of Nightindale.".

Then a reporter, publically broadcasted a rough image of this Robinhood of Nightindale, prepared with help of a sketch artist and a poor from that night. Jay and Jack were glued to TV screens, and hell the sketch looked a lot like Max. This was alarming, as people would now want to know who was it. After all, a legacy was to be made. Max came in between, to take the TV remote and turn it off.

Max said, “Hey that’s enough, less the people see my sketch, better it will be.”.

Jack said, “Hey, its not the same with us, we are the sketch behind this sketch of yours.”.

Jay stood up, “Even I have just made up a sketch plan to catch that woman. Let’s see if I am right.”.

Jay took Jack with him, while Max went in to his study to work from home. I mean, with a sketch going on in public, Max wanted to avoid public as much he could have. The last thing he would want was police or NGO’s stopping at his doorstep asking where he got all that money from. So, it was no stepping out of home. Max had reclined on the chair, and got into thinking, while he was going through few startup pitches. Max was no more scared of that woman, I mean it was her that has given this killer confidence to Max, that he can pull anything off. Especially after this robbery, he felt like a champ. Maybe, this woman would automatically stop, as she would see that it no longer bothered Max. But that was too much to expect of that wretched woman. But seriously some woman was taking too much to her heart, I mean Max now knew it was from those women, and whatever was between Max and them was not that big a deal to piss her that off. I mean, one an ex-girlfriend, one a potential could be wife, one a grand daughter in law of great landlord, one had a crush on her, one sister of brother’s ex-girlfriend, and one a fraud rather a boastful fraud. I mean this was not big an equation to make Max rob somebody of his entire fortune. Seriously, poor Mr. Chester who by now be in his full conscious, regretting on his moves that day. Seriously, how bad he must have been feeling, so tricked, so manipulated. Max prayed that Mr. Chester didn’t suspected Jack. Max’s phone rang.

Emily said, “Hey Max, it’s me Emily. And right now I am looking at that ring you gave me.”.

Max exhaled, “Oh, of course. It’s from Tiffany and if someone even doesn’t sees it, what’s the point.”.

Emily smiled, "I was thinking, that maybe we get again together, and do this again.".

Max hesitated, "Oh no, no, no. I am no longer buying more rings.".

Emily said, "Ha, ha, ha. I am not talking about ring, one is enough for me. But the other thing that fitted quite well, and that was not enough for me. So Viceroy's club tonight.".

Max bite his lips, "Hey, I think I made myself clear that night. That this would be the last and the first time, I was going to fuck somebody. And, I truly enjoyed it too. But we can't keep doing this. I am sorry, but there is nothing between us, and I actually tricked you to get fucked. Trust me, I am not that kind of man, but I truly enjoyed that night, and if you can just only forget me, and forgive me.".

Emily said, "True, there was nothing between us, between our bare bodies. This is not done Max. I am not a whore, I mean you can't do this to me. Oh, you just did, that night. Oh God.".

Max hung up the phone and blocked Emily's number. God, this was all coming back. Shit, he broke a woman's heart whom he had truly appreciated. Wait, what if this Emily goes on to find his home, Stella, and Daisy. I mean all good things Max was known for would end in a blink. God, this was what happened when you fuck with somebody. Karma was calling Max, but Max couldn't have answered it. Emily was done for good or bad whatever. That was an unfortunate night, when a good looking woman met a good looking man. They found each other good looking, and did good things the entire night. Max told himself. God, that was not so good, Max had spitted on her, slapped her, this was not so cool. He had just devastated a woman, who for goodness sake had waited for years for a man to come in her life, and a man did cum, I mean come, but this coming was no good.

God, on one hand people of Nightindale were witnessing a comeback of hero, while on the other a woman was waiting for his comeback. God, no, no, no, he would never return to Emily especially when he had Stella in his life. But seriously, what life, this life was so done for now. Wait, it was not just Stella, but one more woman in his life, and this god damn woman was so not supposed to there. God, what if Mr. Chester also went up to Police Station, and yes he had seen his face, though he must have not been in his all senses, but still. Max shut off his laptop, and then the door bell rang. God, now who can it be, was it Emily, god no, that would be another disaster. Max slowly went up to the door, and stood there while the door bell rang again and again. Seriously, Max had never wanted this much to left alone after that phone call from Emily. He slowly opened the door, to find back his breaths.

Jay said, "Hey, its Nina. Your childhood crush, who is crushing your life now.".

Max turned, "Hey, she was not my crush, I was hers. And they both are not the same thing.".

Jay said, "Whatever, but what remains same is her angst against you. Right from high school.".

Max said, "But why is she trying to make me a man. I mean, I am way past her, I never pretended to be a man to her as I was always sweet but disinterested. Does she think if I become a man, I would find her attractive, or maybe I will stand up to my wrong choices and apologize. Huh. But wait, how do you know its Nina.".

Jay said, "That's like a man, spot on. Now last time, when we heard that Nina's uncles shop was robbed and Victor was helping her with surveillance tapes. It rang to me strange, so I went in again today to ask what precisely was happening. So I got to know, that this Victor has a written permission to access all public areas of city via CCTV to catch the robber. I waited for Victor to go on lunch break, and then with a friend, I saw his history of watching surveillance, and guess what, he has just been following you, and you, and you.".

Max waved his hands on his hairs, "Love is not a crime, but what she has done, is. God.".

Jay said, "My work is done Max. But I know this is not over, so do not worry I am with you, while it lasts. And let me tell you Max, she doesn't loves you. See for yourself, you with me, a detective, a crime detective, and I am with you, as a friend who cares, and a sort of man that loves you too. So don't let her go with this.".

Of course Max wouldn't have let her go now, after all of this. So Max and Jay got back in their car, to meet Victor. I mean getting Victor as an alibi would be the greatest thing that would have happened in all these days. But wait, would Max now report all of this to Police, of course not, I mean what would he tell, that he broke a leg, robbed a man, fired a colleague, fucked a woman, wait that was not illegal, neither was firing a colleague, and then got himself circumcised, wait really his cock's cover was gone, it hardly felt any difference, maybe Max would have got used to it. Anyways, Max was not telling all of this to the Police, to be thrown into a prison. So Victor, it was a public surveillance creep keeping an eye on Max.

They were driving, while Max looked back at Jay and smiled. Jay smiled too, as he perfectly knew what this smile was for, of course catching that woman. I mean Max felt a little bad for saying all those bad things to Jay, I mean he was quite competent, and out of nowhere, no clues, he had found that woman. Oh, wait, wait, wait, she was no longer 'that woman', but Nina, freaking Nina. Why didn't it occurred to Max, that it was Nina, I mean only she had access to public eyes. Of course she had to be. But something was missing, I mean, of course now it was Nina, but she had some other reasons too. Max tried remembering hard, but nothing came back, as in if he did anything rude to Nina, or he said some foul words to her. I mean only a couple of times he had made fun of her, but was that too offensive. Come on, kids do this all the time, and they were kids back then. Jay and Max had now reached the Police Headquarters, where Victor sat. They went up to his cubicle.

Max said, "Making it simpler for you, you pig faced freak. Here I am, out from your public CCTV cameras.".

Jay said, "Your game is so done, enough you have watched us, now watch what we will do to you.".

Victor whiffed, "Seriously, what will you do, apart from screaming in mid of a police floor. I did nothing, but just my job, to watch the entire city for Nina's uncle's shop's robbers. Now if you keep popping on in my screen, I can't do anything. But its interesting, because only criminals pop in such videos. Are you.".

Max yelled, "Here he said it, and what are you waiting for. Arrest him, arrest him.".

Jay said slowly, "Hey Max, I am a private detective, and he is a policeman. So I can't arrest him.".

Victor smiled, "Thought so, by the way, while I was watching for robbers. I came across a video from street outside Mr. Chester's home, ah he too was robbed recently. Found it interesting, and was thinking that maybe I should forward it to my supervisor. What do you think guys?".

Meanwhile, the huge TV screen, on the floor of Police Headquarters had news running on it, and it too popped with a breaking news. It caught their attention and they turned to see the same Harley driver with a plastered leg, shouting at anchor who was holding the sketch of the same Robinhood.

He yelled, "He is the same man who broke my leg. He is no saint, and I bet soon you will hear news of hit and run from Night Square. It is his style, show the money, and then break the leg.".

Max turned back, "You know what we think. We are thinking.".

Jay pulled Max's hands, while the anchor on that TV screen had now switched to full screen sketch of that Robinhood. God, the last place Max would want to be with was standing next to that sketch in a police Headquarter. In fact many brows were raised. Policemen were watching Max and then that sketch, not because that sketch resembled much to Max, of course it did, but the situation of Max yelling at Victor, and that Harley yelling at anchor was just too perfect. Seriously, now what, Max had caught that woman, and also her helping hand, oh helping eye. But nothing to do, no this was not going to end that easy. I mean Nina will have to pay for this, and everything she has been doing. Come on, this was how men were, you hit a man, a man will hit you back. She wanted a man, so she would get a man.

Jay was calming Max, while all on the way. I mean this was just too much, how could this man, wait, yeah Victor could see Max in his eyes while he had helped that witch Nina. I mean no guilt, a dead conscious, and this man was telling Max that he would send that video to his supervisor. Seriously, I mean what world was he from. Jay had stopped the car in front of Max's house, and he kept his hands on Max's. Seriously, this was not manly, but it was way more manly anyone could have imagined, especially Nina. But wait, Max's house door was opened. God, this not be that Harley driver who had traced Max, he thought. They went inside.

Chapter 18

Fred said, "I don't know why, but this sketch looks pretty familiar. In fact I got a copy of it from local police station, to have a closer look, and a voice inside me says I have seen him somewhere, but where, so I came to you.".

Max exhaled, "I don't know, I mean its you who has 100 of friends and not me.".

Fred snapped back, "Of course I am familiar with many, many friends. But not criminals.".

Max said, "So friends can't be criminals, but of course family can be. Right Fred.".

Fred yelled, "Stop fooling around Max. I know we are not on very friendly terms, but I know how you look. This is you Max. What the hell were you even thinking before breaking a man's leg, and where did you get 1 million to give to poor's. I mean what are you even doing, you have escaped your family, for last couple of weeks to do these adventures. You know, I had to hide today's newspaper so Daisy could not see this sketch.".

Max said, "You did right, because Daisy can't know that I had a twin brother whom our dad threw in bin.".

Fred frowned, and smashed the copy of sketch on table to stride out of the room. Seriously, this brother in law needed a lawyer right now, not to accuse Max of these crimes, but to sue him for sheer inequality. Max laughed as he saw the sketch, while Jay was just getting a hang of family drama. I mean Fred never would visit Max's house, unless he has to pick Esther, or he has to pick Daisy, or he has to join a family dinner, or most importantly if he had something against Max. So obviously, he couldn't have missed this chance. But Jay was concerned, as people were starting to get suspicious about Max and that sketch. I mean it also wouldn't have made sense to distribute that money with a face mask on, I mean that was a heroic thing.

But of all, Max shouldn't get caught, I mean this could endanger Jack and Jay as well, who have thoroughly enjoyed making these plans behind the acts. Jay was no longer a detective, but had become a crime advisor to Max, and all thanks to Nina.

By now she must have known that Max knows that it was her. Finally this woman Nina was caught, and this was over. But anyways, it has been good. I mean Max got to fire someone he hated most, Max got to pull the skin of his cock which might have been unpleasant but damn that is how it was, Max got to enact a X Rated movie or maybe wilder than that, Max got give poor people money which he always wished he would someday, Max got to break a leg and be that bad back man. But this didn't meant that Max would let Nina go. Now it was Max's turn, and he needed Jay most for weirder ideas.

Max said, "Now that we have caught Nina, she is not going away that easily.".

Jay nodded, "I was expecting this. But I didn't tell you something, the moment I found that it was her, I went to her home and it was locked. She has been out from home since last night, as per neighbors. I have my men looking for her in entire city. Trust me she is not going away that easily.".

Max waved his head, "Are you kidding me. She is gone since last night, do you think she would get anything easier than these 12 to 15 hours, to get away. God.".

Jay came closer, "Maybe she is sleeping over with a boyfriend. I mean she can have a second crush, right.".

This was unbelievable, I mean second crush. Of course she can have second, third, fourth crush, but what she can't was what she was doing to Max apart from being that childhood crush. Damn, now Nina was missing. Jay went on to get a glass of water, not for him but for Max. Then Max's phone rang.

Nina said, "Hey Max my man, it's me Nina. Of course, now you know that.".

Max snapped back, "I am not your man, and its you who is going to know what I am going to do to you.".

Nina laughed, "Relax Max. Now tell me what makes a man hero of the day.".

Max laughed too, "Ha, you are kidding me right. Seriously, now what is this question for? I thought you will ask, what does a man do to his enemies. Anyways, catching evil people is what makes a man a hero.".

Nina said, “Wow, we are sure tuning in. I mean it was this close. It is killing the villain. Now Max listen carefully, you have to kill a badass criminal who has done no harm to you, but rest of the city. If you don’t, I will get your Uncle Sam killed. I mean he was the protector of your family right. In fact last night few of my men attacked him. He is still in trauma with no clue that his life now depends on his nephew. And Max, Victor will no longer be watching you, so I will depend on news. So the criminal you kill must get on air, or I will have a news of Sam for you.”.

Nina hanged the phone, while Max called Daisy. “Hey Daisy, did uncle Sam got attacked last night.”.

Daisy after a pause said, “He is fine, and thanks for the concern. By the way, entire night Stella has been with Uncle Sam in the hospital. But whom am I telling to, a man who broke another man’s leg for no reason. Fred told me. So I don’t wonder if there be reason that some men tried breaking our uncle.”.

Max said, “Daisy, its Nina. Remember the girl from my school who had a crush on me. She did it.”.

Daisy smiled, “Don’t fight with all women in your life. Or she will walk away too, like Stella did.”.

Daisy hung up the phone, while Max looked at Jay. Obviously, this wasn’t over. Till now Nina was making Max do all these things from her home, but now she was a criminal on run and more dangerous. Wait, who was the criminal here, Max, right. Max now took the entire glass of water and had it in a flow. There was silence in room. Seriously, Jay couldn’t have done nothing apart from calling his network, if anyone had spotted Nina. Despite of doing that, there was nothing solid. I mean the situation was that Jay and Max literally had to catch Nina to make this stop. Now kill a criminal, my god, what kind of manly thing was that. I mean of course the good men killed the bad men, but that was all in cop movies, and for god sake Max was a venture capitalist.

Was this happening, was this real, could shit get that serious. Max was dumbfounded. By the way, Uncle Sam in his younger days had taken care of Max’s family. He was like a godfather to Max, not the criminal type, but the helping types. You know, it wasn’t Charles, Max’s father who got him candies, or that little bicycle, but Uncle Sam. And now Max couldn't have let Uncle Sam died. IN fact, if there was someone in family, Max respected most, it was him. I mean what would Max answer to god, if his uncle died. This was next level, what Nina was doing.

Jay said, "Hey Max, don't worry, its normal. Criminals die everyday, and nobody cares. Even if they don't, they should die everyday, you will be doing good. And I know many criminals, so I can take you to them. Trust me we will sort this out. Its easy killing a criminal, I know, because I have had.".

Max said, "Hey Normal People don't kill criminals, its criminals that kill normal people.".

Jay said, "Max, you are not normal people, you a friend, and an ideal family man. Don't think what Daisy said.".

Max said, "Jay I am thinking what Nina said. And yes I am an ideal family man, the only idle man who is dying for his family, without even a single credit for it.".

Jay said, "I know a criminal, whom the entire city wants to be dead. Now the question is, do you.".

What Jay wanted to say was that he knew a man who was hated by entire city. A criminal whose death will be celebrated, and not even one policeman would care on who did it. I mean what could have been better than that for Max. The only problem was his hired goons who surrounded him day in day out, the people who would die for him, and also kill for him. But then Max was too not alone, I mean Jay was there and he knew exactly what needed to be done to kill this criminal, but seriously, a murder, now Max had to do a murder, god, does any man imagines such a day, or wants to be a heroic murderer. But then, killing a criminal was actually good for all, but then a murder, god no. Max took Jay and they both got riding on his car to see Uncle Sam in Hospital. Well, Max didn't say, but he wanted to see Stella, I mean of course he wanted to see Uncle Sam too, but riding right now was because of Stella.

God, life can take such turns too. I mean Max had lost his wife, lost his sister, and now Uncle Sam who was in trauma. I mean it couldn't be simpler, take a life or lose a life, save somebody or kill somebody. Wow, I mean Nina was a genius, she knew that Max would do anything for Uncle Sam. I mean this woman was so well researched, she tailed Max's sister, Claudia, not only tailed her, but got her hands on a sex tape too, god, this was not a work of a day or two, this Nina must have got behind Max's back least since a year. Max rushed into the hospital, feeling little weird, because last time he saw Stella was walking away, and last time he spoke to her was when Max was trying to fuck her friend. God, Max slowed his steps as they closed Uncle Sam's room in hospital. Max stopped Jay and they both slowly stepped to watch from the window. Wait, Stella wasn't there, and then the nurse told that she had left just an hour back. God, Max took a deep breath, while he sat alongside Uncle Sam who was unconscious.

Max said, "You know it's weird, but back then when I was a kid. I said, that I had two fathers.".

Jay calmed him, "I can understand, even I had two mothers. I mean my father had a girlfriend whom he introduced me to as second mom. Wait, I think it's not the right time to say this.".

Max smiled, "God damn, he was always too good to me. He was my hero, my godfather.".

Jay said, "Max, one godfather has to go, for this godfather to stay. I can put my men here, but it won't stop Nina.".

Max said, "Anyways you put your men here, and I know how to stop Nina.".

Max was in, and the plan was simple. Jay would introduce Max to this crime lord, while what Max had to do was, win his trust, get close to him, and take an opportunity to take him out when he expects it least. Time was less, as Nina would no way wait for months or weeks, to listen the news. So apparently Max had only 2 or max 3 days. He had to do it, and he had to do it fast. This was the only way that Uncle Sam was to live. Now the target was no other than city's most infamous crime lord, Tony Montana. Yes the man, whom everybody feared, the man who was behind half of the city's crime, the man whom no police can touch, and the man who ruled city's streets. Back then when Jay was a police officer, his biggest mission was to end Tony's empire. No policeman had ever dared, but it was Jay who took on the crusade. In fact the mobster that tricked Jay in a bribery case was no other than Tony's own brother. Back then, Jay never revealed that he was on to destroy Tony, and kept everything under the hood, under the cover, by slowly taking down his men one by one, while he was on a very friendly terms with Tony, but Tony's brother Ricky got suspicious and took him down with bribery case.

After all was over, Jay had again patched with Tony, and even did few of his dirty detective work too, to sustain his bills. But deep down, Jay had an ocean of angst against Tony and Ricky. I mean now, Max killing Tony was also fueled by personal vendetta of Jay. I mean Jay would love to hatch a plan to kill Tony. After all it was about what he couldn't do as a policeman, maybe he could do as a detective. Jay drove Max to Tony's headquarters, Fountain Pub, where he sat all day and ran operations of his gang. Again, the plan was simple, Jay had just to find a way to introduce Max as a highly rich man to Tony, rest was all figured. They sat in the car with pub's door beside them. Jay looked back at Max and could feel a bit of fear.

Jay said, "Max these people live on fear. So first you got to cut this fear down.".

Max said, "I don't know why I am like this, I am about to kill a man whom I am feared of. How will it work.".

Jay said, "It works Max, it works. We all kill people we are scared of. But what you are doing is noble, you are going to kill a man, whom everyone is feared of.".

Max coughed, "Hey wait, noble men don't walk into a place like this. But heroes do.".

Jay patted on his back, while he rode out like a boss, throwing keys at the valet, to take a round to be on side of his friend, Max. Nothing had changed, this pub was as shady as it was years ago. Jay could even recognize few of Tony's men, to whom he smiled. Jay had a whole new level of breath, which whistled that unfinished businesses would now settle. It was night and the pub was full, with loud music. But seriously, for Max, all he could see was Uncle Sam lying on that hospital bed, and sooner he got out from there the more Max would consider himself to be a good nephew. It was not about this Tony, but like always about family. The pub had young men, then young women, and then really dirty men watching over. Max could clearly see, guns tucked in pants, which could have his name written on them. This pub was also owned by Tony, and Tony knew Jay as an ex policeman. The odds were too high, but then his friend Jay had too much of faith in his plan.

Prior to this, Max had only known noble men that cured cancer, or established schools in remotest areas, but as per Jay killing this filth was also noble, though again Max would get no credit for it, and he also didn't wanted the world to know, but only Nina. They went up to the lounge section where on couches sat grumpy men, and that Tony in mid of it. He had half naked women sitting on both his sides, and a cigar tucked in between his lips. Tony glanced Jay, and he smiled, while the girls went to the dance floor. Max and Jay were now seated beside Tony.

Jay said, "You know whenever I am scared, I think of you. It's good to have a man for it.".

Tony smiled, "But people tell me, that when they think of me, they get scared. I am a man like that.".

Jay laughed, "Hey Tony, don't flatten yourself. You are not a man like that, you are a man like no one.".

Tony slowly laughed, "You still talk like a policeman, because only cops think I am no one. Anyways, I am sure you didn't came here for no reason, so have a drink and spill it out, ah the reason.".

Jay looked at Max and kept a hand on his shoulder. "He is Max, a friend, a close friend. And someone has been bothering him, well we will talk about that later. More importantly, he wants to get a man killed. He is a nice person and I want him to stay nice, while you get his dirty work done. He is also a rich man, and I am sure he will stay rich, after he pays you for that kill.".

Tony grimly nodded and gestured his finger, while one of his man came forward. Tony said, "He is Clyde, one of my close man. He will do the kill, Max just tell him everything. And you Jay, get it straight, once you step in this club, you are not nice, because I have never been nice.".

They laughed, while they also drank. Tony was getting comfortable with Max and Jay. The girls that have left, had now came back, sitting on their laps. The one sitting on Max's laps, was getting extra cozy. For a minute, Max wanted to throw that girl off his laps. I mean not because Max didn't liked a lap dance, but seriously his Uncle's life was in danger, and he was here to kill a crime lord, and this woman was making Max think from between his legs. God, this was not the time. But gladly, the girls left soon, and some more men came in. Tony got into serious talking with them. As Max could hear fragments of their talk, they were planning on taking out some businessman, and also a drug consignment. Now the time had came for the next phase of plan. Max was only waiting for these men to leave. There it was, they were saying goodbye to Tony, while Max pressed a message send button. A call came on his phone. It was a video call. Max picked it and started talking.

Max said, "Hey Robby, I am sorry I can't make it tonight. I am with a friend.".

Robby said, "Seriously Max, by being here too, you would have been with a friend. Or tell me if I think wrong.".

Max said, "Well, you must know, I don't put my money on people that think wrong.".

Robby snapped back, "Oh but you did this wrong, I mean by not coming tonight.".

They laughed, while Tony caught a glimpse of Robby on Max's phone screen. He scratched his head for a while, and then looked back at Max. I mean Tony had listened all they were speaking. He felt little confused. He got closer to Jay and whispered, "Hey isn't that Robby Dalton the tech billionaire.". Jay nodded, and Tony ordered for a bottle of another champagne, but a much better one. Now half of the plan had worked. Jay had known this weakness of Tony. I mean Tony might have been a criminal, but his real interest was in business, and he always was on a lookout for wealthy investors, who could help him spread his business. But because of his crime record and tainted image, people scared in putting money on him, in fear he would not return back. And now fortune had got Max to his pub, plus Max was in a compromising situation as he wanted something to be done by Tony. Max hanged the phone.

Chapter 19

Tony said, "You have invested in a Billionaire, a billionaire, so what does that makes you.".

Max smiled, "Someone who actually invested in a bloke till he became a billionaire.".

Tony exhaled, "You know what, invest in me. We will do a massacre. Hey Clyde, first things first, find out about every enemy of Mr. Max and kill them, all of them. Because these people can stop your boss becoming a billionaire.".

Max laughed, "Hey no need Clyde, no need. You just need to kill one man.".

Tony laughed too, "Look Jay, he is no nice. But I am not sure if that is him, or that is us.".

Max said, "You know, I am not going anywhere, so we will talk about it. About investment.".

Tony held his hands, "Oh yes, even I am not going anywhere. In fact we all are not going anywhere. Only our enemies will go in ashes. You know Max, I am glad you came to me. Ah, Thanks Jay. Listen Max, Money and power cannot stay away. Money needs power, and power needs money. I'm power, and you're money. We are destined.".

Spot on was the plan. I mean Tony didn't looked right, nor left, but only in Max's eyes, and kept on talking to him. All his men have now blocked off entry to the lounge area. It was just Jay, Max, Tony, and Tony's trusted men. They went on talking. In fact Tony was quite curious to know more about Robby, on how he was, what were his habits, what he liked, and what he disliked. Tony wanted to confirm if he too had traits of a billionaire. Tony was desperate, in fact he was only desperate about one thing, more business. After lots of drinks, Tony confessed, that once he would have a legit business he would leave this crime world, as he was fed up of police, and enemies. Tony wanted to appear on newspapers not because of some new murder, but because of some crazy business deal.

Max couldn't believe that he had made friends that quick with one of city's nastiest crime lord. Tony got up and took Jay and Max for a ride. Tony wanted to show them what all small businesses he had already invested into. The city was not the same through tinted glasses of Tony's car. I mean no one in the city could have even touched Max, for now. The drinks were still flowing in, while Max smiled and even appreciated the Taxi business, couple of restaurants, a butcher house factory, and a dry cleaning business of Tony. God, I mean Tony was really serious about his business thing. But seriously, Max's mind was in the hospital, and what Nina was up to. They stopped at an ice cream parlor. It was Tony's favorite and he wanted Max to taste it too. They were eating some gelato.

Tony said, "It is strange, you are such an influential man, but I never heard of you.".

Jay looked at Max, while Max smiled. "You are powerful, right Tony, but where is your power, ah not the guns.".

Tony looked confused, Max continued, "Because power can't be seen, its felt. Same is with money. I mean just because I am influential, I am not supposed to carry bags of cash with me for shutterbugs.".

Tony laughed and said, "You know there is only thing that can kill Tony, this gelato from diabetes.".

They laughed, while Tony did something that Jay and Max had both not expected. He invited Jay and Max to stay with him for the night. Jay and Max both tried refusing, but Tony anyway took them back to his apartment which was just one floor up the Fountain Pub. I mean Jay hadn't seen this coming, and doubted if Tony was getting suspicious. But seriously, what would he suspect of, Jay was no longer in Police, and even if he finds that Max was a venture capitalist, it would just help them further. But staying in his den was little uncomfortable. Plus Jay had plans to check updates on Nina from his network which too would get delayed. Saying a blunt no, could have ruined their plan, so they went up ahead. Seriously, the last thing Max would want was police raiding Tony's place, and catching them with him. Or worse, Tony's enemies attacking his place and killing them along.

The night went on, while they slept. All Max could remember was Stella walking away, Daisy fighting with him, Uncle Sam resting in that hospital room. You know, it was true that life sometimes did gave you lemons, and so sour that you wont be able to make a lemonade out of it. Slowly the night went on, and someone was trying to wake up Max. It was Jay, they looked at each other, and got walking towards Tony's living room. Wait what was that, I mean not the tea kettle, but guns spread around it on breakfast table. God this was more dangerous than both of them had thought to be.

Tony looked them, "Good Morning men. You both now know many things about me, now my turn.".

Jay hesitated, "That's little concerning, because when your turn comes, people die.".

Tony laughed, "I was so right, I mean Jay, you haven't changed a bit. Hey, now we are friends, you, me, and Mr. Max. I just want to see, where Mr. Max had made his investments. This is man to man, because I want to know how good his business acumen is, before I propose him a partnership. I hope you don't have a problem with that.".

Max smiled, "We have something in common. You kill people, while people themselves die for my investments.".

Tony said, "Argh. People are born to die, while friends live forever. Get your backs moving.".

Max took an excuse of going to the washroom, while in another minute all 3 were down sitting in his car, ready to tour the city again, but this time to see where Max's money was. Seriously, Max had not to lie, in fact Catalyzers had made investments more than that ice cream parlor sold cones in a day. So Max went on, showing him more of his company's manly investment. In fact he would even stop to meet some or other man from the company, to win Tony's trust, who still had two guns tucked in his pants. The first stop was Pharmaceutical research company which both Jeff and Max had invested into on behalf of Catalyzers, but for now Jeff and Catalyzers were out of picture. They kept moving, while Jay was constantly looking back at Max through the rear view mirror.

I mean this was the third phase of plan, and the most critical one. For Max it was do or die. It mean if something happened to Uncle Sam, Max was no good than a dead man. Sometimes you also got to kill for the family, and there it was, the situation Max was in. Max was causally meeting with his old clients, while Tony was getting more n more impressed. I mean the happiness on face of tony was unparalleled, as he was already making sand castles in his head on where all he would invest. For him this was the big game, as all investments Max had shown were big shot. The next stop was a shipping company that had an exclusive area in the dockyard. Jay stopped the car while Max explained Tony everything about this business. Jay looked out, and nodded.

Max said, "So Tony, this is where it ends. I mean, its one of my biggest investments.".

Tony said, "It's all in your hands Max. I mean to change the status quo.".

Max smiled, "I haven't done anything like this before, especially with city's nastiest crime lord.".

Tony nodded, "Trust me, I will be the last crime lord, you will do this with, because I won't let you go.".

Max said, "Everybody has to go Tony. Anyways, as I am here, I will meet my friend, and be back in a minute.".

Max and Jay got moving towards the office of this shipping company. Both were smiling, I mean the third phase of their plan was just on verge on its glorious completion. Tony was sitting in the car, and had lighted a cigar, while Jay and Max kept moving. I mean seriously, it was just last night they had met Tony, and now there they were. Max and Jay got on the door of the office, while Jay nodded, not at Max. Shoot, shoot, shoot, heavy round of gun fires started, towards their car in which Tony was sitting. Un stoppable, bullets after bullets, straight for couple of minutes. I mean Max's car was right now smoking, and all they could see was bullet holes. This was the third Phase of their Plan.

Max and Jay went back towards the car, to see Tony smudged in blood with so many holes in his body. Tony was killed. Max smiled, on the fact that he had got city's nastiest crime lord killed within 24 hours. I mean even the police and FBI have been on his lookout for decades. This was faster than Pizza delivery. I mean god, Tony was killed. The dockyard had echoed with sounds of gun rounds, but there was no one to listen. Max and Jay turned around the car, while Clyde had got in to see the dead body. Wait, was that Tony, Clyde pointed gun at them, while Jay had too taken out his pistol to point at Clyde. Everyone got still.

Clyde said, “You prick, you cheat, you fraud. Who are you police, FBI, Homeland.”.

Max said, “Call us whatever you want, but we are going to call you, Tony’s killer, if you don’t turn around, to walk away like any of this never happened. By the way, all this shooting has been recorded, and Ricky would love to see it, and know what happened with his brother.”.

Jay said, “You have done your job, so you will get your money, and also a new boss. So cheers.”.

Clyde said, “I did a mistake, a big mistake, but trust me, you will too, if that video comes out.”.

Jay and Max both showed a thumbs to Clyde, while he walked away. This was Phase 4, the last one, to sort out the hand of killer. Now Max had got a crime lord killed who has done no harm to Max but all the city. This news had to go on air, so Jay quickly called couple of TV news channels, and most importantly Ricky to tell him that his brother has been taken out. Now as Max was saying, they had a video of Clyde shooting on car, actually Max had two videos. One from an angle where Jay and Max was were standing near the office while car was being shot, this video they showed to Ricky, via this shipping company records rooms, the other which they didn’t was from the opposite angle where Clyde was shooting at car. By the way, since last when Tony had ordered Clyde to follow Max’s instruction, the plan had started. While this morning they were headed out, Max went to the washroom to call Clyde to shoot at a car in shipping dockyard, once they stepped down. Poor Clyde had followed Tony’s and Max’s orders, and there they were.

Max and Jay were walking clean, and already back in their home to turn the TV on, which was now flooded with News of Tony Montana been killed. I mean seriously, what a senior police officer with all the resources couldn't do, was done by a friend, couple of venture capitalist and a private detective. Max had just liberated this city from clutches of crime. In this act, Max's biggest concern was that he didn't wanted to murder a man, and it was then that Jay came with this plan;. Winning Tony's trust and luring him for investment was crucial to take him out this day, alone without his bodyguards on a ride. Jay knew he would, once he trusted Max. I mean Max did felt like a hero, a more smarter hero, who can kill the villain with their own weapons. The TV news went on.

The anchor said, "A dark era of Nightindale has ended.".

Another anchor said, "Tony Montana was not a name, he was a feeling we call fear.".

Ricky Montana on TV said, "When he killed my brother, he forgot to dig a grave, for himself.".

A TV discussion said, "A Robinhood kind of man appears and donates money to poor. 2 days don't pass, and then Tony Montana is found dead. Is this a chain reaction, or our city has a new hero, a hero who is working in shades, and doing all good things. And actually it makes sense, a villain has died, so a hero must have been born.".

A policeman on TV said, "Thanks god, it is the last crime which will have Tony's name in charge sheet.".

Max couldn't help but smile. I mean this was crazy, as everything Nina had made him do, eventually gave Max a sense of satisfaction, despite of the fact that all these were wicked acts, or dirty acts. God, I mean this was his childhood dream of maybe killing a villain, it was killing the Death Vader. I mean this was something Max should have shared on his social media profile, but wait it was too risky, as killing someone was still a crime as per law of this city. But this was also cool. I mean Max didn't even kill him, but made him die. But seriously, Someone had to keep an eye on Clyde, to see he doesn't opens his mouth, but then he won't, as when this video would come out, he would be the first person to die.

Max had already called the hospital to check, and his Uncle Sam was discharged, and already having Pies in his home, as his cousin told him. Of course Max hadn't called Daisy, as she would still be mad at him. She just needed time to forget all this, for things to be normal again. But of all things, this had to end, I mean Max couldn't live in fear of been caught for a robbery, or been taunted by a woman whom he fucked, or being exposed for killing a crime lord. God, where was this Nina. She had a very small family as Max remembered, I mean where could she go. She was hiding, so obviously this wasn't over, and she was not in a mood to patch up with Max. Anyways for now things were good, to be called a Hero, again and again by so many people that too on National TV. Jay was talking with someone on phone, while Max called him to just have a look at the TV.

Jay said, "Max I have a bad news. Nina was spotted at the city airport.".

Max said, "I think its good news, as Nina was at least seen. We do have a lead on her, right.".

Jay said, "Ah, its still a bad news as we do not know where she was headed.. But trust me, we are on her.".

Jay got another call, and went on talking, while Max kept on watching the television. In fact Max's boss had also called, to tell him that he did good by meeting all those clients, despite of fact that Max wasn't told to. I mean these were the men that kept Catalyzers rolling. God, it seriously had been long, though Boss hadn't complained about Max been missing, but seriously, tomorrow he was straight going to office, and no more becoming the hero of city. Nina was seen, so chances were she would be caught soon, so all of this would end.

Max couldn't wait to have his life back as normal. God, I mean these past few weeks have been the craziest phase of his life. Wait, did he just became a complete man, of course I mean, fucking a woman, breaking a leg, robbing and donating, killing a criminal, I mean there wasn't any thing significant left to do, unless Nina had some other creative ideas. Wait what was that, why was Jay shouting on phone, why was he getting hyper. Max slowed the volume of television, while Jay quickly moved on towards the window, and hanged up the phone.

Jay said, "Here it is, another bad news, Ricky's men are now keeping an eye on us.".

Max approached, "It's not a bad news, I mean nothing has changed. First it was Nina, now Ricky. Huh.".

Jay said, "Max, everything can change from now on. Ricky had got me down once, he won't hesitate again.".

Max nodded, "You know what, man to man, we have got his brother down, and we won't too hesitate.".

Jay exhaled, while both got back into the room. I mean of course, no matter how many clean video you show to a criminal, he won't believe that the last person his dead brother was with have nothing to do with his death. Wait, not just a criminal, but any man. So now, here was another man behind Max's back, trying to find the truth. But he wont be able to prove anything, as Max didn't even owned any gun, nor any contacts with mafia, so how would he get Tony killed, and on top of that, Ricky didn't knew about Nina, so apparently Max had no reason to kill Tony. But wait, a brother of a dead crime lord won't prove anything, he would just get them killed. God, now this was getting tricky, and dangerous. Wait, what if Ricky now targeted Max's family, god no, that would be the last thing he would want. Anyways, what Max had to do was just stay low, till all of this got over, and Ricky went back to business as normal.

For a minute Max actually regretted for not having called the police when Nina had asked him first time to fire Oscar, that was a big mistake, to have actually taken things light, and believe that Max did hated Oscar. In fact Nina hadn't done anything wrong, she had just made Max's wildest dreams come true, yeah that was it. Maybe something was wrong with Max, maybe the discrepancy was in Max, not in Nina. She just made well use of every thing that Max always wanted. God she knew everything about him, his likes, his dislikes, his weaknesses, his strength, his vulnerabilities, and his dreams. I mean kudos, for doing a good homework. Meanwhile, on TV news, something caught Jay's attention and he slammed his head with his hands.

The Harley Driver said, "This is the same god damn car, which that man was driving, who broke my leg, and I am sure he is the one who got Tony Montana killed.".

The news reporter said, "As per statistics, 1 out of 89 people in our country have the same car.".

The Harley driver said, "Oh wow, I didn't knew that. By the way how many people are in our country.".

The News reporter turned back, "It's all getting connected. A man breaks a leg, out of his whim, then a Robinhood appears, and within 2 days Tony Montana is killed, while in the car he is killed is the same that was ridden by man who broke a leg. But he is still my hero, at least for slamming a man who doesn't knows our population.".

Jay said softly, "Seriously, Nina would be so proud of you, after seeing this.".

Chapter 20

A man with a broken leg, another man with an empty safe, a criminal killed, a woman fucked, a colleague fired, a vulnerable cock, and bunch of poor people with lots of stash, was what Max was left with, and these all people were now coming back. I mean there was no going away. They were now haunting back Max. This Nina has now given Max a new past. I mean Max now could nowhere be seen in Whimshire, nor in Chumswick. From now he could not have made friends with another crime lord, he never wanted to, but now even if he changed his mind, he couldn't. He couldn't now take Stella to Viceroy's Club on a date. For Max it was end of driving to Night Square after evenings to grab a good cup of ice cream with Esther. I mean, these people were everywhere, and Max couldn't have risked it. Maybe this was the cost to be paid for becoming a man, apart from all he was going to pay to Jay, and to the car dealer for a new car. Or maybe this was the cost for making fun of a girl who had a crush on you, in an age when you didn't knew anything about Karma.

God, was life unfair, well someone should have asked Max about it. One mistake, and your life could become like this. I mean what if Max had taken Nina seriously back then, and dated her, or took her to restaurants for couple of times, maybe slept with her too, and all of this could have been avoided. I mean Nina was never odd looking, she was good, but only a little weird. But then these times were weirder too. Meanwhile, Jack too had dropped by Max's house, and they all three were sitting and sipping beers. Jay's network was on work, while Max was praying in is mind for this to end happily. Then Max's phone rang.

Nina said, "Hey Max my man. Guess what, this is the last time I am calling.".

Max said, "Ha, ha. Will we miss you, no. Because guess what, we are going to catch you.".

Nina said, "But what will you do, once you catch me. What's done is done, you can't change it.".

Max said, “You are wrong, changes happen. See now I am a man, and you know what angry men do.”.

Nina said, “I don’t know what angry men do, but tell me what does a man do to mark his territory?”.

Max laughed, “God, you are unbelievable. I did it, and you are already out of your house, ah territory.”.

Nina said, “Now listen very carefully Max. You have to challenge a top notch politician to do a street fight with you. You have to intimidate him to be compelled and fight with you. Beat him with all you got, and tell the entire city, on who is the man. If you don’t then Jose would not get admission in his ivy Law school. I have a video of Jose addressing anti Semitism secret society that i would send to the admission team, if you don’t do it. And you know a law school wont admit somebody already prejudiced. So, hurry up Max, for this last one.”.

Nina hanged, while all of them were now looking at Max. Max for now was muted. By the way, Jose was a law student, and was on course to do his post graduation. It was his only dream to become a lawyer, ever since he had known what to become. Jose had worked all his way to get good scores, which he had shared only a month back. Everything was on track, but now if Nina shared that video with admission team, or made it viral, the bar association could also have blacklisted him even before he became a lawyer. I mean his career would be doomed. His life would be finished. But for a young brother does an older brother needed to fight with a politician. Of course, Jose was in this situation only because of Max, because of Nina, and Max had to do something.

God, no, again, and now beating politician, a top notch politician. I mean how could Max pull this off. He could go on to jail for this, I mean not necessarily, and his career would not get endangered too, as many would see it as a manly stuff, but Jose would be finished. His little cute brother who still had that baby soft skin.. He would collapse and would not be able to bear all of this. God, wait, there was no other way, Max had to do this. Max received a short video on his phone, and he played, while Jack and Jay saw it too. It was Jose, and wait was he wearing that Nazi shoulder band too, oh yes he was. This was limits of carelessness. He was hurling abuses on Jews, and Max stopped it. Max called Jose.

Max said, “Hey Jose, are you sure that you want to become a lawyer?”.

Jose felt confused, “What happened brother. Of course I do, and you know that.”.

Max said, “But I didn’t knew that you also wanted to bring Einstein back to life to cage him and to work on Time Machine, so that you and your anti Jew friends could go back in time of world war 2 and make Adolf Hitler win it. You know Jose, this too is a serious job, as good as being a lawyer, and way tough than becoming a lawyer. You still have time, so think about it. And yes let me tell you, this one is so cool.”.

Jose smiled, “You know, Einstein’s body parts were misplaced, just to avoid such scenario.”.

Max yelled, “Shut up you idiot. The first thing you will do is break all ties with that secret society. No questions asked, or very soon you are going to need a lawyer, not become one.”.

Max hanged the phone, and felt pity on his brother, and pitiful on himself. I mean seriously, what a crazy family Max had, one sister was having sex in front of camera, while brother was talking about bringing back Einstein to life to only enslave him. God, but how did Nina got her hands on these Country got Talent videos. I mean she was tracking his siblings, god that was sick. I mean she had got the entire family into this scene. I mean seriously, no one could have seen this video. I mean racism was a serious crime in these times, and how did Jose not think about it. How silly of him. Anyways, Jose was a good brother and would sure listen to Max. Now the bigger things at hand were to street fight a politician. Max stood up and sat on couch in between Jack and Jay.

Max said, “You know people wish to be a politician, and not to beat them that too publically.”.

Jack said, “Max, this is how history is written, a Man versus a top politician in a street fight.”.

Jay said, “A Man versus a politician, seriously, what school you went to, and what history you read.”.

Jack snapped back, “A school whose annual day isn’t preceded by a politician.”.

Max said, “God, now will I have to beat a politician, that too not in an election but on street. But she said, this was the last time, and I cannot fail Jose. And seriously, the history I have had in this past few weeks, this looks easier than an annual day performance. I mean I just have to beat him, and fights happen all the time.”.

Jack said, “That’s like my man. Now the target is a politician, so you get to vote. Let’s choose which one.”.

Jay didn’t said a word, as fights happened all the time, and who could know this better than Jay and Jack. So they all got working on which politician was Max going to challenge. This was tough as Nightindale was the capital of this state, and in fact there was a whole neighborhood in the city which had a politician in every other house. So in total, the choices were many, and Max had to just pick one. In fact Jay too got excited as they got started, after all he was going to be a part of plan to beat a politician to whom probably he had saluted for straight five years. The first thing they did was do Google search on list of politicians that lived in Nightindale. There it was a list of 90 plus people. They started with the most prominent ones.

The first was Minister of state for Health, Benjamin. Jack insisted that he was a good target, as he was quite someone in his 50’s and would be easy to beat, plus the people of city were always angry at him for the worsening situation of healthcare, I mean Max would be praised for beating him. But Jay declined, as he would never volunteer to fight, and Max’s attempt would go in waste. Then there was Minister of State for Finance, Ernest. Ah, Jack got again excited, as he was infamous for not responding to public pleas demanding on expenses of government. Jack had a personal enmity with him as he too was an accountant and he thought that Ernest was no good in finance. But again Jay said that he would never take up the fight. The list was now getting short, as prominent ones were less.

Then there it was another name, Minister of State for Youth Affairs, Travis, a young chap, who had been a wrestler in his younger days, but quite infamous for his corruption. In fact people of the city hated him. Jack didn't got the best feeling, as he was physically good, but Jay gave a nod.

Jay said, "This man will easily buy your fighting challenge. He was wrestler, and won't mind getting in a fight.".

Jack snapped back, "Of course he won't mind, because eventually he will beat our friend more.".

Jay said, "Relax Jack, Max has just to fight, and beat him. This is not about some trophy.".

Jack said, "He is your friend Jay, not because he wants discounts in your bills. Getting it.".

Max smothered Jack, "Hey listen, Jay is right. I just have to fight him, and what if he gets to beat me too. The history will only remember, the common man, the man, the Max, who was also a good friend of Jack. Now listen, put some extra efforts on our friendship, or you will lose your place in history.".

Jay said softly, "Max you have my nod on him, but let me tell you, he is dangerous, and not a good man.".

Max said, "I know, but Adolf Hitler is more dangerous, and I cannot let my brother win him WW2.".

Meanwhile, the television behind them was featuring a news piece that Travis will be doing a road show, this evening in the city. Wow, I mean the stage was set, all the people will be there, not because of Travis, but the Mayor and other ministers would also be there. Clearly, no one would mind seeing Travis getting kicked in back. Most importantly, people would not label Max as a villain, plus the wrestler inside Travis will surely have confidence in himself to have a fight. Plus, Travis was already going under a trail of bribery case, and if Travis beats the shit out of Max he would have an upper hand, and a public sentiment which could win him the corruption case. So chances were that their plan would work. Max, Jay and Jack were now seeing all together the news piece, they knew it, that this was the place, this was the time, the history was going to get written, ah not history, but the chapter Nina would get closed.

They waited for evening to dawn. Then there it was. Max, Jay and Jack were now sitting in their car, while the road show getting warmed up. Max had a feeling from inside that he can do this, and beat Travis. Jack was thinking that his friend would become a hero for sure now, while Jay was thinking what would follow next as Travis would not sit quiet. Whatever be the reasons, but Jose was sure going to the Law school. All three of them had spread in different directions to dissolve in crowd. That was the plan, to be divided, yet stay united. There he was Travis, meeting and greeting people along with few of his party members. God, beating a politician, come on, wasn't it always what politicians wanted, of course, so it was all normal, Max thought.

Travis said to crowd, "Lovely people of my city. I Travis, pledge here to bring jobs, reduce unemployment, create more youth centers, reduce the standard college fee, raise standard of education, create more community centers, all for you people, because youth is the voice of this city, and the future of this city.".

Max shouted, "And of course corruption in between all of them.".

Travis saw him with amazement, while Max shouted, "Standard of education, my foot. We understand how you have managed a BMW, and a house in Blooms Arcade without a college degree.".

Public also started seeing Max, while Max shouted, "There is no future of this city with you.".

Jack from other end shouted, "Beat the youth out of this Travis. Show him, how a young punch feels."

Jay shouted from other end, "Tell this Rep cock sucker, we all are in this together.".

Max pulled off his shirt while now the crowd was also roaring. "Man to Man, Travis. You think you are our leader. Not mine. You must have fought many elections, now fight a lovely man of this city. The youth of this city wants to see, what you have got, apart from ability to pimp votes.".

It had worked, and Travis murmured, 'That's it'. He was clearly intimidated, while Jay and Jack kept supporting Max with cheers, which had now amplified, as public too wanted to see Max beat the shit out of Travis. Travis had told his party member not to interfere, and he too had pulled out his shirt and got on the street face to face with Max. Travis jumped on Max, while Max punched hard on his flying face to slam him on ground. Travis felt disoriented, as he had clearly underestimated Max. Max kicked him hard in his stomach. Travis stood up looking around, and now he had realized that he had made a mistake. Clearly Max had nothing to lose, he was commoner, but not Travis.

Travis kept looking around to see if people were on his side, and Max punched him had to make his face bleed, again and again, while more people took sides with Max. Travis had totally lost it, and he couldn't even turn his back. While the News reporters were telecasting it live. Travis was so dead, as he thought, while Max wrestled his arms around Travis's neck to give him a slam dunk, Bam it sounded, Travis's body crashing the street. Max heard it and was sure, Travis's bones have started breaking. Max then jumped on him with a nudging elbow, and damn people would hear Travis moan. This was ugly, the police tried interrupting, but people stopped them. Max lifted Travis up, to hold him and slap him again and again. He kicked him hard to throw him to the other side.

Max yelled, "Rome was not built in a day, but Roman empire can be brought down in one day.".

Wow, Jack was on cloud nine after hearing this. People were all sticking close to Max, as if they had got their new leader. People were kissing him, smothering his hairs, while he walked. Jay and Jack had joined him too. While Travis laid there, to be eventually picked by party members, who too were clearly disappointed on how badly Travis an ex wrestler was beaten. All the other leaders, were taken back to avoid any further face offs, while the common people of the city were celebrating in mid of streets as if it was their road show. Max again had emerged out to a hero, a hero who now owned this city, and its people's hearts. Media was al trying to take a bite of Max, who didn't even had a scratch on his bare manly body.

A news reporter said, "This is the most manly thing of this entire century. We want to hear you.".

Another news reporter said, “This was not just a fight, but stance to take sides, and people have taken theirs.”.

Another reporter said, “Alleged bribe that Travis took, will sure now come in handy for his healthcare.”.

A reporter said, “Max is clearly the hero of the day, but was it Max too that killed Tony. Because clearly as per Max and what happened, we can see, there only can be one hero in this city.”.

A common man yelled on camera, “This is a message to DC that do not mess with us. We are Max.”.

Jay and Jack had that winning smile, while Max joined them to head back home. God, this was so done, and Travis was so beaten up. I mean it must have been so unexpected to him. Jay was now feeling better because media had covered it all, so Travis would not do anything stupid. Wow, so this Nina thing was all over. Finally Max felt like if he was man. I mean he was born a man, but now he had passed some sort of test to certify that he was a man, in fact all of the city now knew that he was a man. I mean Max belonged to a family of immigrants, and he had just beaten up Travis whose ancestors have been this country’s oldest landlords. Wow, that was ironical, and this country had accepted him too. I mean all the kisses of those people was a testimony to it.

Home was feeling home again, and it was good to be hanging out with two good friends. Max looked at his phone and smiled, as he knew that no more satellite calls were going to come. God, it all felt like a dream, a distant dream, that every man dreams of. The television was turned on, and why wouldn’t it be, I mean the entire media of this country and city was playing the same footage of Max beating up Travis, while in Max’s house beers were all opened, and Media had started to gather outside his house. Jay had suggested Max to keep it low, and not make any statements. Wait, that can’t be true, the man with broken plastered leg was again back on TV.

The Harley rider said, “This is it, he is same man who broke my leg, and now has beaten our Minister.”.

The reporter said, “Come on he was warming up, or would you have seen this day.”.

The Harley rider said, “Oh, glad to hear that he was warming up, or I would have not seen this day.”.

Jay switched the channel, while the Head of Republicans was making a statement, “Events following this day had led us to disbanding Travis from our party. He has no right to get in a fight with a man, a common man whom this party has ever stood up for. Here is the resignation letter of Travis, which I hold in my hands, by the way he too could have, saying which that he is fine now. He no longer will be Minister of Youth Affairs. And also I want to clear the rumors that we are not taking in that man Max, in our party, because someone needs to be on streets too.”.

Chapter 21

All's well that ends well, someone has rightly said. Everything was getting back to normal, except for few Media OB vans that were clouded outside Max's house. I mean why wouldn't they, Max was the latest sensation in the city. In fact last night, Max's boss had also called in amazement on when did Max turned bulls from a venture capitalist. It was not just his boss, but many old friends of Max were now turning up to catch up with him after seeing his face of fury on Television. Boys and girls of entire neighborhood were glued on their terraces, and balconies to get a glimpse of Max whom they have only seen driving in and driving out. Max was not sure, but he knew that somewhere, Nina wanted to devastate Max, but what happened was opposite, he became a hero, and a better version of himself.

I mean people of this city was now talking about him, Max did this, Max did that. And for now Max was not bothered, if people knew that he was the Robinhood, or it was him who killed Tony Montana. In fact it was better if people knew that, as it was good publicity, but wait why would Max want publicity, maybe to be remembered in modern history of this city. But of all, Max was little dazed, if his beating up of Travis would be liked by Stella or not. I mean she was more of a peaceful woman. But Daisy for sure must have jumped off her seat, to see Max in action. Seriously, the friends he was with were best ones, but still Max was missing his family, especially the fury face of Fred just because he could in future have befriended Travis, but Max killed the chance of it. Ha, such a typically idiot Fred. Jack was cooking the breakfast, while they were seated back. Max's phone rang.

Fred said, "Max, you must be feeling great, I mean beating a politician doesn't happens every day in our life.".

Max said, "Oh, I am. Also, it doesn't happens everyday that Fred gives Max a call.".

Fred said, "You know what doesn't happens every day, Daisy getting assaulted while on her way to super market. Yes your sister, and you know why, because her brother has gone crazy, beating people, breaking legs. You know Max you might have become a new hero of this city, but you have failed your family.".

Max snapped back, "Hey is she okay, tell me who did this. Fred just wait I am coming.".

Fred snapped back, "No need Max, she will be okay, if you just tell the media outside your house that you have no family. In fact you do so, we all will be okay."

Fred hanged up the phone, while Jay and Jack approached Max who hurriedly takes the back door to get in his car. God why didn't Max see this coming, Of course this was a possibility down there. These people knew, while Media is with Max, they cannot do anything, but they could always harm Max's family. God, why does always family has to come in between. Max was driving at full speed, and has already broken two signals. Jay was quiet, and knew that nothing could calm Max now. I mean Daisy was attacked, not Fred. I mean Max had just got over with Nina, and now these criminals and corrupt politicians have got started. God, Daisy must be so scared, and all of it because of Max. And seriously what about Esther, she must be terrified to see Daisy scared.

Max had to stop this, and the best way was to be with his family. Max stopped the car in front of Daisy's house, but it was locked. God, Max tried calling Daisy, and then Fred, but both disconnected the call. As if now Max was the bad guy, I mean no matter what the entire city was thinking, but for them Max was the bad guy. But Max couldn't have left them alone, so he drove back to his parents house, as of course they might too get in trouble. It has just been week, that Charles had got a liver transplanted, he would be too vulnerable to any goon attacking him.

Nina, Nina, Nina, what have you done, was what Max was thinking. Of course it was all because of this wretched woman that his family was in danger. What was happening now, was no fun for Max, he stopped the car at his parental house, god damn it, this too was locked, and Charles nor his mother was picking the call. Where are they, wait, no way they are been abducted. Max got into frenzy, and his head started spinning. He was losing his ground. Then his phone rang.

Travis said, "Wondering where, Daisy, Fred, and your parents have gone. Right Max.".

Max yelled back, "Hey Travis, don't test me. You have picked the wrong people.".

Travis snapped back, "You did wrong by picking me, Max. Now listen, all your family is on way to Fred's country house. Trust me, because my men are following them. But I am not sure, where next they will be headed to.".

Max said softly, "Travis leave them out of this, I hit you, you hit me back. I am right here.".

Travis said, "Max you didn't just hit me, you also hit the people I represented. Now its my turn, I will not just hit you, but also the people you stand by. Just wait for your turn.".

Travis hanged up the phone, while Jay tried calming him down. God, making history was never that simple, because history is written over corpses. God no, if anything happened to his family, Max would for sure burn entire DC down. Wait, Fred's country house was 1 and half hour drive from here. Max took Jay, and got seated in his car, to head to Fred's country house. Max was sure that Fred even wont let him enter the house, but least Max could guard the fences. God, what was happening. This was so not done, wait, what about Stella, god, she could too get hurt. Max called Stella, but she too disconnected. Her house was close by, so Max made a quick dive to warn her, or probably take her along to Fred's country house. Everything Max had stood for was falling apart. While driving, Max had already alerted his cousins and Uncle Sam to keep themselves grounded in house for couple of days, and he would explain everything later when he drops by. Everybody in Max's life was in danger, Max even looked back at Jay, while Jay gestured to the gun tucked in his pants.

Wait, Jack was alone back in home, Max tried calling him, but he too didn't picked the phone. God damn it, why were people not picking his phone, was this some new sort of phone virus. Seriously, was it only Max who was bothered. Max had now reached Stella's house, but it too was locked. Max took a deep breath, and thought maybe Daisy must have taken her with them. Max's phone rang.

Jose said, "Brother were are you, some people have attacked me, a while ago. I somehow escaped.".

Max closed his eyes, "Hey listen Jose, everything will be fine. You just go back in your hostel and stay locked.".

Jose said, "Brother, it was where I was, but they broke in, and now my room is a mess.".

Max with heavy breaths said, "Okay, go to some of your most unlikely friend, and stay there. You know these are good times, to make friends with least expected people. Okay, think good, and I will call you.".

Jay said, "Hey don't worry Max, I have a police friend from town Hall, who can watch Jose's back."

Max said, "Come on Jay, do you think a policeman can stop an outraged politician. But still give a try.".

Here, there and everywhere, were troubles coming for Max. I mean this Travis had got Max running like a mad bull. Now Max was driving to Jose's place, to take him along. I mean he couldn't be more safe than being with his brother. Seriously it was better that Jose didn't went to Law school, least his life would have been safe now. All of this because of that stupid Nina, who thought beating a politician would be fun. Max was already thinking on how to stop Travis. His mind was racing, wait, what if Max appeared on the same media standing outside his house to speak a public apology to people that probably he was drunk then and out of his sense when he beat Travis. Maybe Travis would be taken back in party and he would forget all of this.

Would it work, or should Max go on to the same media, and shout that this Travis was now trying to kill and finish all of his family, wait that would for sure worsen things. Wait, Max's boss from Catalyzers had a republican friend, maybe he could bring some sense to Travis. But this was too personal, and he would never listen. Max was driving fast to town hall, but in between he would forget where he must drive to, to Fred's country house, to Travis 's house, or to Town Hall. Max's phone rang.

Ricky said, "So Max, how does it feels to see your little brother getting attacked.".

Max stopped the car and said, "Hey Ricky, he is a nice boy. And this is between you and me. Please.".

Ricky said, "Oh, if he is nice, then I am sure my brother Tony would get a nice company up there.".

Max yelled, "Hey Ricky, no, you can't do this. Just leave him alone.".

Ricky said, "Listen Max, I can do this, and seriously what I can't leave alone, is my brother Tony.".

Ricky laughed and hanged up the phone, while Jay consoled him that if Ricky's men were behind Jose, then his network could for sure keep a watch on Jose's back. Jay assured him that if anything happened to Jose, he would put a lock on his detective business. Max and Jay were now returning back midway from town hall. Max was getting a little better to hear that Jose will be safe, but a little worse to hear that Ricky too now was after Max's back. I mean this had to happen one day, and Max knew despite of the fact that he never paid attention to it, but Max knew. God, I mean there was no other way of stopping this other than fighting these people again, and again till one of them go finished. This was the only way. I mean no words of this world could bring sense into a mad politician, and a rouge criminal. Maybe this was time that Max took police protection, but what if then Travis pressed assault charges on Max, and Ricky files a case against max for killing Tony. I mean all the people hailing Max as hero would then vanish. This was how world worked. Max's phone rang again.

Claudia said, "Hey Max, I think there is some crazy man after me. He has a broken leg.".

Max exhaled, "God, Claudia are you okay. Don't tell me he did anything.".

Claudia said, "Yeah he did, I mean he slapped on my butt, but then I turned and slapped him back thrice on his face. Then he yelled at me, fuck you Max's sister, and then my boyfriend came in and took him to parking.".

Max said, "Don't worry Claudia, he is an unfinished business. Let me see what I can do with his other leg.".

Max took sight of relief, and told Jay to keep someone look Claudia's back. Thanks God, he didn't did anything wrong with someone's sister. Wait, no, what if Emily got back into the picture, god, no way, and what if Junior Chester was already thinking of ways to bring down Max. God, Max thought, these were enough troubles for now. One day, and Max's life had changed upside down, I mean for past hour he has been driving zigzag in the city, changing his destinations after every other call he received. But seriously, how did that Harley driver got Claudia's address. I mean was he able enough to ride to Williamtown.

Was Max a man now, well it seemed that nobody cared anymore. Now a freak Harley rider was slapping on his sister's butt, wow that was the day Max was living for, all because of that one woman Nina. His life was becoming a disaster. I mean Max wasn't even sure if he will be able to meet all of his family members again, will they be safe, will they be alive to have a thanksgiving dinner again, all of this because of one woman Nina. I mean where this would end, Max standing on dead body of Travis, or Max standing on Massacred gang of Tony, or maybe in prison for all of this. I mean was Max still a venture capitalist at Catalyzers. He hadn't left the job, but no more he was the same person. He was changed, in fact this change started right when he first time had fired Oscar for no reason. This was where all this madness started. Meanwhile Jay received a call, and Max couldn't help but notice his excitement. Jay was smiling as he hanged the phone.

Jay said, "A good news, after all. We have a location on Nina.".

Max stopped the car, "Ah, good news for us, and bad news for her. But still a news.".

Jay said, "Max now as you have turned the car, I hope our phone doesn't ring again.".

Max snapped back, "Oh yes, but I have no more family, and I hope Nina has nowhere else to go.".

There it was, what both of them were hoping for but hadn't said a word about it. I mean what could be better than finding Nina and telling all these people that it was her who made all this happen, now fuck her, beat her, kill her, break her leg, steal her house, do what ever you want to. And this was what exactly both were going to do. By the way Nina was spotted at an old house in Belltown, it was a neighboring country side of Nightindale. So it wasn't even that far. Nina was staying at this place since last two days, and one of Private Detectives Association had spotted her, in a grocery store, and immediately he did a face match with the WhatsApp circulated picture and gave a call to Jay. So now, these people after Max's family were just to be convinced that they should avenge with Nina.

It wasn't going to be easy, but Jay had already started the talks while Max was driving. He was calling one by one to Ricky, Travis, that man with broken leg whose number he got from a media friend. In fact he had also called Mr. Chester and Emily. Max was opposing this, but Jay's idea was to have maximum people at the scene, to have diverse reactions, with a greater possibility that these people held Nina responsible for it. The plan was simple, while Nina had no idea that it was now her turn for troubles. Max and Jay stood outside the house Nina was supposed to be in. Jay's men were already keeping any eye on her. Of all the bitterness that had grown, Max still had a soft corner for Nina and wanted to ask her, on why she did all of this. I mean maybe Max had missed something, or did something wrong to her. Before Ricky, Travis, Mr. Chester, Emily, Oscar, and that Harley driver ate her away, Max wanted to have a word, so he went in along with Jay, in this on the verge of falling down house.

Max said, "What. Uh. What the hell are you doing here Stella?".

Nina came in the living room from another room hearing his voice, "She is my cousin, Max. By the way, what the hell are you doing here? We didn't invited you.".

Max stood there stunned, "Stella, get up, and better get going, things are going to get worse here.".

Nina said, “This is the man I was working on, who cannot even take care of his fiancé and her cousin.”.

Jay interrupted, “Ha, ha, Nina, this man has already taken your care, that you will soon find out.”.

Max went up to grab Stella’s hands, while Stella said, “Relax Max, Now as you are here, let me tell you a story. Once upon a time, there was a happy small family that lived in a small village of Kingdom of Isles. There were two brothers, David and Daniel, and their exceptionally beautiful wives Emma and Sophia. Though Emma was more beautiful than Sophia, but it was all in the family. One day their neighbor who had gone out of country returned, to tell them what fortune he had made. He said that across the seas, there are heaps of gold, that only needs hard work to be earned, and would look good on beautiful women. Life was there across the seas, this family knew, and they were tired working day and night, to meet their needs. They had to build a better future for their generations to come, so they sold everything they got and got landed in a foreign country with dreams in their eyes, and belief in their muscles. David and Daniel were everything a good master would want, and so they soon got a job. But every day when Emma and Sophia would come to hand them their lunch, their master would feel jealous, that how can his servants have a more beautiful wife. So he fired them one day, telling them he hates anything that is more beautiful than what he got. David and Daniel couldn’t do anything, while their master ensured that these both didn’t got another legit job in the city. So soon they started working in a local bar. Months passed by, and they were earning good, so one day a local goon who was always jealous of expats thought why should an outsider have a bread which belongs to one of their owns. So he broke David’s legs. Now a family of four, and one man to earn the bread which was Daniel. But it wasn’t just this, the goon had now convinced the bar owner that foreigners didn’t deserved to sit beside us, but clean our gutters, and water our dishes. So the bar owner made Daniel do the same with much less wages. Meanwhile a rich landlord had got his eyes on Emma, the most beautiful woman he had ever seen. He proposed her that if she sleeps with him, he would send 6 months of ration to her house, and get her husband a job which couldn't happen without his influence. Emma thought it was just about one night, which could give her family bread while they again stood up on their feet. So she slept, but that rich landlord fucked her, fucker her hard, and this forcibly continued, till David got to know about it. After all they weren't even that poor, and David thought of selling all the gold he had got. He went to the jeweler and they decided an amount which would end all of their troubles. But the brother of the Jeweler, came back one night to steal all of the gold David and Daniel had. The place they lived in, used to laugh on them. One day, David and Daniel decided that they no longer will be out ruled, so they went ahead and contacted all the expats from Kingdom of Isles to create an association. But the rich landlords couldn't bear it, so they got Daniel killed. David was now broken despite the fact that association was now created. But then one day the locals of this city along with their leader came and broke David's little office, and thrashed every other man of this association, along with David, so no other foreigner would ever raise their voice against them. David couldn't bear any of this any longer, so he along with Emma and Sophia left the city, but not the country. But you know the people that had devastated their lives, kept living on, on and on.".

Chapter 22

While Stella was telling this story, Oscar, the Harley Driver, Emily, Mr. Chester, Ricky, and Travis had arrived. They were all listening to it very carefully, and knew exactly about all the characters she was speaking of, while Daniel, David, Emma, and Sophia looked them boldly from the hung family picture in living room.

Stella said, “I just wanted to give a little morality to this story. And I did.”.

Max said, “You made me do all of this, just because something bad happened to your family ages back.”.

Stella said, “Yes Max, and you did all of this, so something bad didn’t happened to your family now.”.

Stella continued, “We are same Max, we both love our families. But I wished, if you were my man, a man who would care to know about his woman’s family, where are they, how are they, what they have been through, and all of that. But you know what Max, nothing is more important to you than your own family, and my family was never yours.”.

Travis interrupted, “Hey, hey I was just wondering, who was that rich landlord, that fucked Emma, because right now, I feel like if my blood is calling me.”.

Travis pounced on Stella, while Max came in between to stop him. Others too followed, to have a piece of Stella, but it was Max only Max in between them and Stella.

Ricky said, “What’s your problem Max. Both these women are now ours, isn’t that what you wanted.”.

Mr. Chester was yelling, “Does this house have a safe, because that is the booty I’m interested in.”.

Harley rider said, “You broke my Harley, my leg, and now you are breaking my heart Max.”.

Emily got in between, “Hey Max, listen I don’t want these woman, but you.”.

Oscar stood in a corner, “Max seriously, your fiancé needs to get a job.”.

Stella took out a gun, while Nina followed. She was now pointing gun at all of these people, while Max in between was trying to calm them all down.

Max said, "Stella, this is not who you are, and you already have your revenge.".

Stella smiled, "Max you know nothing about me. Okay do you remember that night when you made fun of Nina while she gave that lovely card to you, of course you do, you know what I was standing just besides her. That was the first time we saw each other, and I knew that someday this boy would do anything for me. Because poor Nina had a crush on you, but you were just checking me out. I have tracked you, I have followed you, known everything about you, and it was then I decided to come in your life. You still think you know me.".

Max said, "I don't care, what I know is that we are going to be good together. I can fix this.".

Stella shot a round on roof and still pointing guns at them, "I don't want to, I want you to screw them Max.".

Ricky pounced to hold Stella's hairs, "Max's innings are over sweetheart, now we'll do and you'll see.".

While Mr. Chester yelled from his place, "But I still don't see a safe in this house.".

Emily held Max's hands, "Max I will forgive Stella, but you just forget her.".

Max struggled through the bunch of crowd, and got hold of Stella. I mean there it was, the unshakable love that Max had for Stella. He was still trying to protect her. In fact Max was thinking that he made a wrong move, by calling them all in one place, only because this all was done by Stella. But Stella didn't gave a damn to all these people including Max. For a minute, Max thought that all his engagement with Stella was a lie, and just a means for Stella to have her revenge. Everybody was going out of control. On the other end of room, Nina had picked a chair and was shooing away by swaying it to anyone that was trying to come closer to her. Max got hold of Stella.

Max said, "Hey Stella, did you ever loved me. Now is the time to tell.".

Stella smiled, "Oh yes I did, especially when you were fucking Emily. Ah, I swear on my great grand mother Emma, at that moment I did loved you, and I knew that only my man can do this.".

Max blew his breath, "Okay, Okay, but why did you got me circumcised. Was that revenge too.".

Stella said, "You still don't know me Max, I like it raw. Ha, ha, ha.".

Ricky jumped in to point gun at Stella's head, "Oh I have something better waiting for you in heaven.".

Stella was laughing madly, while Ricky had loaded his gun to take a shot. Max yelled at Ricky to stop. For a moment time had frozen. Max tried stopping Ricky, but his hands were all tied by Travis. Wait, but then the police came in. Well, the moment Jay and Max had entered this place, Jay had seen Stella, and known what they had planned was not going off the shelves. He knew this would get tricky, so he had called the police. The best bet to keep Stella the woman of Max, safe and sound. Everybody took a step back, while policemen got spread all over the place. They arrested Stella and Nina, while another policeman was calming the crowd. I mean was this the end Max was looking for. God, it was her own woman that didn't even think that Max was man. God, it was Stella. All this time, he felt special because he had to avenge his woman. Max looked back at Stella, and clearly there was no regret. I mean the way she was acting, it felt she was proud, but Max knew that she was broken, what Max didn't knew was if she was broken because she was caught or was she broken that she had lost Max. I mean, all of this that Max did for his family, was actually for Stella's family.

He could see in Emily, his rich great grandfather who did wrong by misusing his place in society to fuck Emma. He could see in Ricky, his great grandfather who was discriminate towards immigrants. I mean, Max too was immigrant, and if this all had happened with his family, he too would be mad, he too would be angry. But what Stella did was ruining his beautiful present for her family's ugly past. But then this was what family did. I mean Max wouldn't have done the same, but he would have least done something. Max was not mad at Stella, I mean she had her reasons, and Max was just the instrument, I mean it was Max who called himself Stella's man, so being Stella's man also meant that Stella's problems were his, Stella's enemies were his, so Stella wasn't wrong anywhere.

God damn it, Max still thought that Stella was right, maybe it was his love for her. I mean he did everything that Nina said, but for the first time, Max actually felt like a man, I mean a man who did something for his woman. Max too didn't regretted it, but the way it happened was just wrong. All this time, Max had cursed Nina, but it was Stella that deserved both his love and hatred. The policemen were taking both the women, while Max was still not feeling right.

Nina said, "Ha, He did all of that, and we are getting arrested.".

Nina continued, "And Max, what did I made you a man for. I mean did you even get any of it. If you still think you are a man, then rise up, and accept your mistakes. Save your woman. I know you want to do that, while I am just giving you words. Stella is going, going forever.".

Max said, "Thanks Nina, for all this to make me realize that I am man enough, man enough, to let it go.".

Months had passed by, and things were getting back to normal for Max. Max was back in business, to fund the most promising startups. In fact it was just a week ago that Max had won the prestigious Money maker of the year award, because three of his funded startups had shown five times capitalization, and tons of profits. Max was again happy with his life, though at times he missed Stella, but the memories of becoming a man often subsided it. Uncle Sam was as fit as ever and was now pressurizing Max that he gave them a good news of Junior Max. Everyone in Max's family was now loving Max more than ever, especially after the Stella truth came out that Max had done the dirtiest of thing just for his family.

In fact, Fred had put aside his enmity and had started taking out Max for dinners with his friends from high places. It wasn't just this, Fred had almost convinced Max to leave his wall street Job, and join him in a new business venture. Max was not sure, but he did saw potential in Fred's ideas, plus having your own business meant more family time. Remember those women from Max's past, oh yes, Max was now all in good terms with them, especially with Nova whom he had got a catering contract for Catalyzers. It just didn't end there, Max went a step ahead to get Nova catering contracts of all his funded companies. Nova had clearly forgotten all bitter history, and she no longer wanted her house back. With turn of few events, Lucy was again dating Jose, or one might say, Jose was again dating Lucy. It had nothing to do with Max, but recently, Max, Ember, Lucy, Jose had gone out for dinner. Clearly Ember had forgiven Max, and realized that Jose and Lucy both were old enough to take their own decisions without the influence of their families.

Remember Aspen the fraud graduate, she was now been admitted to finish her graduation legitimately in city's best Finance University, whose education was sponsored by Catalyzers under their new program, 'Bring Women Back to Work'. Well this one had lot to do with Max, and Aspen now treated Max as her older brother. Seriously, Max was still as popular as with public as he was months back. Half of the town now recognized his face. Today was again a Saturday and Max was sitting with Daisy, Fred, Charles, and his other family member, and having a healthy brunch out in sun.

Daisy said, "You know every family needs a man like Max. He makes it look better.".

Charles said, "True, he got me a change of Liver, which means more drinks to come.".

Their Cousin said, "Yeah and he needs family too, I mean his own family, not yours Daisy.".

Fred said, "Hey, soon Max and us will all be one big family. He and I are thinking of starting a new business together, which also means more of family brunches to come. Hey by the way, Esther won a piano paying competition yesterday. She won a gold medal, a gold medal. Isn't that great.".

Their cousin said, "Yeah its great, unless you take gold out of that medal for your business.".

Fred said, “Ha, ha. That was the poorest joke I ever heard, maybe our family does needs gold standards.”.

Max went on to the next room, to watch television, as his meal was done, while the family had got started. It was funny, that this ritual of having family brunch together on every last Saturday of month was started by Stella. I mean if she only wanted revenge, why all this drama of getting close to us. Wait, is that Travis, God no, Someone from neighborhood had thrown a bottle of black ink on Travis’s face, as he was out on a road show. God, was this another Max, well whoever he was, he did looked angry at Travis. Max kept on turning channels, while his phone rang.

Anna said, “Max, I need to do some dress shopping, so you get your back here to pick me up.”.

Max smiled, “Hey sweetie, you look good without dresses, so we won’t need them.”.

Anna laughed, “Ha, ha, Max. I know I do. But I am not sure, if you will be good without me.”.

Max interrupted, “Okay, okay. I am getting there. There is no need of leaving me again. I mean I am a man, not an addiction that gets on your nerve every other day.”.

Anna said, “Seriously Max, last time you left me, but this time I will make it even, so hurry up.”.

Well, of all the women from past, Anna had came back better than before. I mean they had again started dating, but they hadn’t moved in together, and this was Max’s decision as he didn’t wanted to repeat the same mistake again. Though Anna didn’t felt so right about his decision, as there was no point of dating if they weren’t going to move in together, but Max just wanted things to go slow. So here was Max again riding back in his car, on whims of the woman in his life. I mean, nothing much had changed. Max’s phone rang.

The woman said, “Hey Max my man, how have you been.”.

***